Alpha Varsity

Renee Rose

RENEE
ROSE
claimed by love

Want FREE books?

Chapter One

Lotta

The approach of a full moon is making me light-headed.

No one can sit still today. No student in Wolf Ridge High wants to listen to a teacher on the afternoon before a full moon run.

Especially not for the subject I teach. Art isn't remotely revered by the shifter community. It's considered a human thing–pointless. Pretentious. Which is why I got the hell out of here as soon as I could.

Every class today has been a nightmare, but this last period–the class with the hulking alpha-hole of the school, Asher Martin–is the worst. He and his football buddies sit at the back table and heckle me.

This afternoon, the smell of teen pheromones fills my classroom, and I'm as restless and horned up as my students. My skin prickles with heat. There's a slow pulse between my legs that I haven't felt in years. I haven't thought about sex this much since I was a teen walking the Wolf Ridge High hallways. Which, admittedly, wasn't all that long ago.

I clear my throat and infuse as much alpha command as I'm capable of into my voice. "I'm waiting for your full attention."

Of course, the last to stop speaking is the deep, swagger-infused voice attached to my nemesis. He turns a baleful look on me. I'm disconcerted by how striking those hazel green eyes are against his tanned skin. How his long and thick lashes frame them. The way they pop under the swath of sun-bleached hair that falls across his forehead. He's in need of a haircut although I'm sure the shaggy length that curls up at his nape and around his ears is a conscious choice. Part of his rebel-without-a-cause persona.

But Asher's disdain isn't just for show.

I viscerally feel the linebacker's hate for me. It burns my skin. Takes my breath when he sends a blast of it my way.

I'm careful to hide my reaction. I may be smaller than many of the students in this class, but I'm their teacher—at least for the rest of the school year. I have to maintain alpha status in my classroom, or I won't survive.

I force myself to stop shifting from foot to foot in my high-heeled sandals, widen my stance, and put my hands on my hips.

Asher's gaze flicks to my legs, and the sight of them only seems to make him angrier. His eyes track higher, and he glowers at my breasts.

I'm careful not to give any attention to his table as I speak. "Yesterday, I asked you to think about what medium you will use for your self-portrait. Today, I want you to write a paragraph describing what you've chosen and how you plan to execute your vision. If you don't know or are having trouble deciding, sign up on the board for a five minute consultation with me about it." I point to the numbered slots on the board.

"Also, everyone should have turned in their charcoal drawings by now. I'm missing three. If they're not turned in by the end of today, you will get a zero on the assignment, which will affect your grade." I steel myself to look at the back table. "Those of you who need to maintain a C in order to play in this weekend's game might want to think about that."

I shouldn't even warn them. I should just knock their grades down and let them suffer the consequences. But something in me still doesn't want Asher to fail.

I make brief eye contact with him, but the anger blazing in his gaze is too much to hold, and I quickly look away.

He was unnerving as an angry, rebellious thirteen-year-old. Now that he's twice my size and carries the dominance of an alpha wolf, that rage is more than intimidating–it's downright scary.

He folds his arms across his chest and lifts his upper lip in a snarl. "I turned mine in."

My gaze bounces back for a moment and narrows. It's a lie. Asher hasn't lifted a pencil in this class since the day I took over for Margarita Adams, the human art teacher who went out on medical leave two weeks ago.

He's daring me to call him on it.

I frown and point at the loose pile of drawings on my desk. "Find it and show it to me."

He slowly unfolds from his chair, making a show of his size. Making me feel the full force of the extra foot in height he has on me. The hundred-pound difference in our weight. The solid sculpted muscle that wraps his long, sturdy bones.

He's an incredible specimen of manhood–and that's not just the full moon talking. Fate may have fucked him with a shitty, abusive father, but it's been kind to him in the looks and size department.

He saunters forward, and I pretend I don't register the threat, even though everyone in the room with shifter blood feels the pulse of his aggression.

I keep space between us, walking to the window to draw the shade against the afternoon sun. There's a predatory edge to his movements. Despite his size, he has the grace and agility of a large cat, rather than a wolf.

He starts shuffling through the charcoal drawings on my desk.

I stay near the window, angled toward him like any cornered animal, ready to bare my teeth if necessary.

After he sorts through all of them, he turns to me and lifts his brows. "You must've lost it, Ms. James. I turned it in yesterday."

Fuck that. I'm not about to let this kid bully me. He may have a legitimate reason to hate me, but that doesn't mean I'm going to let him push me around in my own classroom.

I draw myself up. "I don't lose my students' artwork. That's a zero for you, Asher. I'm sure Coach Jamison will be disappointed when you can't play in this weekend's game."

"Well, he can redo it today, can't he?" Remi, one of the cheerleaders who hangs on his every word, interjects.

I press my lips together. "If it's done by the end of the class, I will grade it." I glance over at Asher's two buddies at the back table–Sebastian and Markley. "That goes for you two, as well. On my desk by the end of class, or you won't have a passing grade for this weekend's game."

Asher strolls back to the table where he reigns and sprawls in a chair. His large body fills the space, spilling in all directions. He looks at me and smirks, as if he's just won the confrontation. A dimple on each cheek winks at me, sending a chill down my spine.

Because no matter how devastatingly handsome he is when he smiles, I know with total certainty he's dangerous. He was born into a violent family. There's violence in his eyes. In his gait. In the feral way he eyes me now.

Once upon a time, I thought I freed him from that cycle of violence, but it seems all I did was cement a sense of betrayal. A hatred so deep, I fear it will consume him.

If I'm not careful, he may exact his revenge on me in the same way his father did.

* * *

Asher

Hate lust.

That's the only accurate description for what I feel for Wolf Ridge High's new art teacher.

I make a purposeful mockery of the drawing she requested by the end of the class, dragging the piece of charcoal around in scribbles on the page. What is she going to do? We'll say it's my definition of art. Markley and Seb follow my lead and do the same.

They know why I hate Carlotta James, the hottest and most talented teacher Wolf Ridge High has ever had. The pack princess who has every male wolf in the school–students and staff alike–running to open her doors or carry her art supplies.

I'm not immune to her fairytale heroine perfection, with her black hair and pale skin and those big cornflower blue eyes that I once believed were full of kindness. But she's the reason my mom and I have no status in the pack, despite me being a huge alpha wolf. She destroyed my family–something I will not ever forget.

I stroll up to her desk after the bell rings and make a show out of arranging my drawing in the center of it, facing her. I'm crowding her space.

I'd like to say it's just to intimidate her–which I know is working–but there's more to it. There's the fact that I'm desperate to get her scent up in my nostrils again, even knowing the firebomb that will explode in my belly as a result.

The approaching full moon has me extra sensitized, and the hit I took when I came up to her desk earlier wasn't enough.

Because I've never smelled anything so enticing in my life. Honey and jasmine and that unique signature that is only hers. I picked up on it the moment she walked into the art studio two weeks ago as our long-term substitute.

It entered through my pores, affected my physiology, and made me realize the horrifying truth.

The worst possible outcome.

Fate decided to fuck me in the ass by pairing me with the one female I cannot stand.

"Write your name on it, Asher." She doesn't look at me as she pushes the drawing my way. She doesn't know. Female wolves don't recognize the scent of their mates as easily as males.

I tap the drawing with my middle finger. "You'll remember who it belongs to," I tell her.

It's a warning. I'm daring her to fail me.

She won't.

Because amongst the notes of fear I pick out of her scent, I caught something else–guilt.

Good.

Lotta should be sorry for what she did to me.

And I intend to make her suffer every day for it.

Chapter Two

Lotta

The hairs at my nape stand on end. My fingers tremble around the stem of my paintbrush, making my lines jagged and rough.

The jade wolf eyes on the six-foot canvas stare back at me with accusation.

Wolf Ridge High is dark except for my art room–the only place I have right now with enough space to paint on such a large canvas. I prefer to paint in daylight, but with the new teaching job, that's impossible. *Temporary* job, I keep reminding myself to stay sane.

I attempt a few more strokes, but the trembling keeps messing up my lines.

Fuck it. Creative genius isn't happening tonight. I drop my brush into the glass jar of paint thinner.

The yips and howls of the pack out on their full moon run carry down the mountain and through the cracked window, sending goosebumps racing up my arms.

Why?

Am I supposed to join them? My stomach knots into a fist.

I haven't been on a full moon run in over four years. I don't know if the fist-feeling is my wolf, angry for not letting her out, or my gut telling me not to do it. That if I indulge in my true nature, I will lose all my dreams.

Wolf Ridge will become my permanent reality. The four colorful years of art study in Chicago will wash out into nothingness like the paint on my brush. I swish the brush in the jar, watching the blue swirl before the entire jar's contents turn to gray.

That's how my life is beginning to look since I returned. My plans muddied and stained. Tainted with the pains of the past.

The howls grow closer. The pack shouldn't be off the mountain, but it sounds like they're coming this way. Probably Wolf Ridge High students, eager to mark their territory on campus.

My legs start to shake. I look out the window.

Don't do it, artist-me growls.

She's fierce. More fierce, even, than my wolf.

It took me nine months to master keeping my wolf in while living among humans in a big city, but I did it. My hair grew dull, and my complexion sallow. I lost ten pounds, which I didn't have to lose in the first place. My parents begged me to come home, but I refused. Not even for the summers. Because once I had my wolf suppressed, I couldn't chance her getting a taste of freedom again. I'd have to go through withdrawal all over again in the Fall. It wasn't worth it.

Now, though, I'm getting hot and feverish. The need to get out there and join my pack has my feet dragging me to the door.

I feel like crying and puking at the same time.

"I can't," I moan out loud, catching the doorframe to stop myself from leaving the studio.

It's no use. I sense the change coming over me. If I don't strip out of my clothes, I will rip them. It's like being a teenager again.

I strip off my clothes in the dark hallway, shedding them piece by piece as I run for the back doors.

I barely make it there before I shift. My two front paws hit the door handle, and the door swings open. I burst out into the cool fall air. The urge to run has never struck me this strong. I race down the football field, staying on the shadowy side in case any humans are driving by. Dirt flings from under my paws as I round the turn that leads out of the schoolyard.

I race up the hill, keeping to alleyways and back streets until I hit pack land. My wolf led me straight to the pack. Without any conscious thought of my own, I fall into position at the rear. I don't recognize any wolves, but it's been a while. Even as a teenager, I didn't let my wolf out often.

We run up and around the mountain, climbing higher. After a stretch of no-thought, one appears in my head.

It's pleasure.

Deep, deep pleasure. It feels incredible to run this way. To be my wolf-self. To feel the rocks under my paws. The bionic strength in my legs. The breeze across my muzzle.

And that makes me want to weep. Like I've betrayed artist-me.

But I quickly forget because a male wolf shoulders me, shoving me off to the side.

I turn and snarl at him. He's a huge black wolf with a white patch of fur on his chest and around his face. His green eyes are strikingly beautiful. His scent is unfamiliar to me, but it tickles my nose, intriguing me.

He shoulder-butts me again, shoving me off to the side, away from the pack. I bare my teeth. He nips my hindquarters, showing his dominance.

My body instantly responds, not with submission but with heat.

Everywhere. It tingles and pools in my belly. Floods down my inner thighs.

He nips me again, and my core contracts. I'm suddenly aware that I wouldn't be able to resist if he tried to overpower me.

When he tries. My belly flips as I suddenly realize what this is.

Courtship.

Wolf-style.

The excitement, the heat I feel, is my body's response to him. My wolf wants this. She wants to be overpowered by him. Not to submit easily but for him to work to win her submission. She's *thrilled* by the idea.

This must be why human females love BDSM. The zing of danger amplifies the sexual excitement. I don't know this male at all. He's huge. Powerful. And he's chosen me. He could do anything he wanted with me, with or without my permission.

He nips me again, driving me away from the pack and cornering me against an outcropping of boulders.

I start to turn to show my teeth, but he strikes fast, tackling me to the ground.

I don't recall my brain giving the order to shift, but suddenly, I'm in human form, pressed to my belly on the soft dirt, with a massive man at my back. Did *he* command the shift?

I turn to see him–I need to know who I'm about to have sex with–but he catches my hair in his fist and holds my head in place. "Uh uh. Face to the ground, little wolf." His voice is hard. As cruel as the grip on my hair.

Moisture leaks between my legs.

I've never been so turned on in my life. I hardly know what to make of it. Is this my wolf's doing? But no, I'm in human form, still turned on.

Desperately aroused.

I would do anything this man told me to do right now for the satisfaction of his touch. His dominance. I feel the nudge of his hardened cock draping between my thighs, and I part my legs for it.

"You want that, little wolf?" I hear a note of satisfaction in his deep growl. He's still holding my hair tight, pulling on my scalp.

"Yes," I pant.

"Yes?"

Does he sound surprised?

"Yes, you want me to fuck you?" he clarifies. I'm in love with his deep voice.

He's asking for consent. He may have chased me and tackled me to the ground; he may be pinning me in place and not allowing me to see his identity, but I do have a say in the matter.

He's not going to take without my permission.

Is this what I want? I must be crazy. This is exactly the scenario I vowed to avoid when I agreed to return to Wolf Ridge for the rest of the semester.

But only one small part of me wants to say no–that voice warning me that this is how I get trapped in Wolf Ridge. I'm doing exactly what my parents wanted me to do, and once I settle into the pack ways, I'll never leave again.

But at this moment, I don't care.

All I care about is knowing what it feels like to be penetrated by the virile male behind me. Receiving the full experience of lust. Of hot, full-moon sex. Of whatever this male wants to do with me.

"Yes."

* * *

Asher

I can hardly believe my ears. *Carlotta James wants to have sex with me.*

It's all I can do not to slam immediately in and ride her rough until I explode. I have years of pent-up lust packed into this moment. That's separate from the years of anger and resentment over her betrayal. Add in the fact that the moment I caught her scent at school, I realized the undeniable truth: that she's mine, and it's a recipe for total combustion.

Yep. Fate fucked me again.

She paired me with the one female I never wanted to see again.

So my blinding need to drive into the delectable body beneath mine is as much from rage as it is lust. This is going to be a hate-fuck.

But that doesn't mean I won't make it good. I keep my grip on her hair and shift my knees inside her legs.

I already know she's ready for me. Even if she hadn't just parted those sweet thighs and lifted her ass, the scent of her nectar would've told me.

"Up on your knees," I order.

I'm as shocked when she obeys as I was when she said *yes*. Then again, her body must know its master. She recognizes the scent of her fated mate.

I just have to keep her from seeing my face.

Carlotta rises to her hands and knees, arching her lower back to present her gorgeous ass to me. I smack it hard. Under the silvery moonlight, I see my handprint bloom on her pale skin.

"Ah." Her cry sounds like a mixture of protest and desire. Her dark waves spill across her back.

I stroke her ass, smoothing away the sting. Then I smack her again, harder. The position of power I'm in right now has my dick as hard as granite. I never in a million years dreamed this moment would come. Me, behind the girl of my former dreams. Her, in complete submission to me, trembling for it.

I don't even have to hold my dick to guide in. It's like it knows its way home.

Carlotta is tight, but she's also sopping wet, the petals of her sex opening to receive me. One thrust, and I breach her entrance. Another, and I'm to the hilt. She cries out with the second thrust, my length no doubt stretching her slender channel.

Carlotta has always been petite, and she seems even thinner since she returned. I weigh twice as much as she does, easily, and my cock is... well, let's just say he's *more than eager* to be inside her.

I stay in close, my loins pressed against her soft ass, and give her tiny thrusts to get her used to my size. "Yeah?" I growl, pushing her head down instead of pulling it back to give her neck muscles a break. I keep hold of her hair, though, so she won't turn to see my face. "Is this what you needed, little wolf?"

She only whimpers in reply, telling me it's still too much.

I slow down even more, keeping my hips glued to hers, only rocking them to slide a few centimeters in and out. With my free hand, I reach around and find her clit.

I barely brush it, and her knees come off the ground, her hips pressing back against mine to take me deeper. The tight walls of her core contract around my dick, drawing a short groan from my lips.

"Did you just come?" My voice sounds more ragged than I want it to. The shocking pleasure of giving her satisfaction so easily is still ripping through my body. I regain my control. "I didn't say you could come. Who said you could come before I do?" I pull out and start smacking her ass fast and hard. "You don't come before me. Not unless I permit you. Understand?"

She doesn't answer–not that I give her much of a chance. I keep on spanking her. "If you want your pleasure, you wait until I give it." I stopped spanking and grip her flesh roughly. I give it a shake. "This ass belongs to me. It's mine to do with what I want. And if I want to spank it until it's red and sore before I fuck you, that's what I'm going to do."

My words are more genuine dominance than dirty talk. They spring from almost five years of anguish at what Carlotta did to me. From my frustration and having my world torn apart and my life ruined by her only to find out *she's* the female fate chose for me.

"Okay." She sounds breathless. Her arousal drips onto the soft dirt between her knees.

"Mmm." I rub the slick flash between her legs. "Did your spanking turn you on?"

She doesn't answer.

"Next time, I'll let you touch yourself while I spank you, and if you're a good girl, I'll let you come."

I don't know why I'm promising a next time. I don't know how long I can keep Carlotta from realizing who I am. As soon as she does, it's over. There's absolutely no chance for us.

Not that I want a chance.

I push into her once more. This time, it's even easier. Her body is more welcoming. Wet. I've already plowed the way open, and now she needs me as much as I need her.

Spanking her settled me. Released a little of the aggression I was afraid I would bring to sex. Now I'm able to close my eyes and savor the sensation of being deep inside her.

Now I'm able to move slowly in and out, measuring her ability to take more.

I build a rhythm, ramping up the speed, plowing deeper. Putting an accent on my in-strokes. A snap to my thrusts. All the while, I hold her in place with the fist in her hair.

"Okay," she pants again. "Okay."

I slow down. "*Okay*, what? *Okay, I need to come*? Or do you want me to stop?"

"I need to come!"

Fuck.

For some reason, that knowledge undoes me. My nostrils flare. I buck against her gorgeous ass, losing the leash on my control. I know I'm going too hard. It's too much. Her knees lift off the ground, and she braces all her weight in her arms to take me.

I don't care. I'm taking what's mine now.

The moon goddess seems to circle us like she's celebrating bringing us back together after tearing us apart.

I'm lost in a hurricane of pleasure and deep satisfaction. That sense that this is where I belong, that everything in my life has been focused on coming to this one pinpoint of a moment. Like this is the apex of my entire life's journey.

I want it to last forever. I know it can't. This fleeting high will be the unattainable measure I claw and scrape to hit again every day for the rest of my life.

My balls draw up tight and start to pump. Almost too late, I remember to pull out.

"No!" Carlotta sounds almost offended. Like she, too, was on the brink of ecstasy. I fist my dick and give it two tugs before I come all over her ass.

"No," she sobs.

"I know." My voice is rough and guttural. "You didn't get to come." I reach around and stroke her clit. It's swollen, the little nub standing out from the hood. Even though I'm still catching my breath, I force my shaking digit to be gentle. I take a slow gander around her clit.

Her exhale is another sob.

One more circle.

She starts to buck her hips.

Halfway around the third, she comes. I shove two fingers inside her, so she has something to squeeze around. Her orgasm continues, muscles squeezing, her hips undulating and jerking. It's magnificent.

She collapses in a limp heap when it's over.

That's when I mentally freak. Because my instinct is to cover her body with my own. To wrap my arms around her and kiss that sweet-smelling, slender neck.

But I can't. I won't.

I release her all at once, shoving backward at the same time I shift, praying she doesn't catch sight of my human form.

My brain tells me to leave her. To run fast and catch up with the pack. Or better yet, disappear, so there's no awkward moment back at the pack hall with her trying to figure out who I am.

My wolf won't let me. It would be ungentlemanly to screw my mate and then leave her while she's still on her knees. I nudge her with my snout to get her up and moving. I don't mean to be affectionate. It's the last thing I want to be with her, but I end up licking her ear.

Then I get a grip on myself. I nudge her again, and when she still doesn't move, I give her thigh a tiny nip.

That sends her into action. She shifts into her wolf form—a sleek white wolf with jade green eyes. I can't help but notice how our wolves complement each other. My large black a match to her small white. Both of us with green eyes. Her wolf is slender, but elegant. She stands for a moment, her head swiveling in the direction the wolf pack left, then back toward the way she came.

To my relief, she veers away in the direction she came.

I watch her trot away. She moves slowly at first, as if her legs don't remember how to work. Then she gains her stride, and soon she's bounding down the mountain as fast as she was running when she arrived.

Good. She's not interested in knowing who I am.

In that case, there may be a next time.

The idea of stalking her late at night, fucking her hard from behind, and never letting her see my face is not just deeply satisfying–

It might be the only way I survive the rest of this year.

Chapter Three

Lotta

I run toward the rear of the school, my body still alight from what happened on the mountain.

I can't believe it. I've never had sex on a full moon run before. I never even had the desire. Tonight, I was incapable of refusing that male from the moment I caught his scent. I wanted sex like I've never wanted it before.

Ugh. This is why I didn't want to shift.

I didn't want to give into my wolf nature and get entangled here in Wolf Ridge. Yet, I can't deny how satisfying it was to allow my animal side out. And I don't mean for the run although that felt amazing, too.

I mean the wild, rough sex.

I'm still feverish and hot. Trembling with desire for that male. Both satisfied and needy at once.

Who was he?

I kind of love that he didn't allow me to see him. He doesn't want me to know who he is. That means he's not looking to tie me down here.

And he was careful with me. He pulled out, even

though I desperately wanted him to come inside me. He had more control than I did.

He's older, perhaps. Certainly far more dominant.

What does the intense reaction I had to him mean? He's not—he can't be—my mate.

Or is he?

Fuck.

If we're mates, he would've recognized it first. Males have an easier time identifying the scent of their mate than she-wolves.

He would have known it the moment he picked up the chase.

Yet he didn't want me to know who he was.

Does that mean he's already mated?

Oh, Fate.

The idea turns my stomach. Did I just have sex with another woman's boyfriend or husband? That's disgusting.

But of course, if I'm his fated mate, he wouldn't have been able to stop himself. Not under the full moon in his wolf form. No matter his commitment to another female, the full moon runs reveal our most authentic nature. We can't stop our urge to hunt. To screw. And if nature shows us our true fated mate, to claim.

This is where the human lore about werewolves comes from. The idea that we turn into monsters who can't stop ourselves from killing is partly true. It's just that we don't kill humans. We hunt game. We stalk the opposite sex.

This is exactly why I tried to suppress my wolf side. I can't be this out of control.

But I should be glad, I guess. If that male truly is my fated mate and is already bound to another female, it would provide me with an even stronger reason to get the hell out of Arizona as soon as this substitute teaching contract is up.

And it would mean he wouldn't stop me or follow when I fled.

I shift to human form when I reach the school's back door. The deep, rich scent of that male still clings to my skin. He smelled of leather and spice.

Standing here naked in human form brings everything back even more cutely. My nipples tighten. Moisture leaks between my legs. Shifting to wolf form brought on my rapid healing abilities, but I still feel the tingling of his spanking and the twinge of the soreness between my legs. I still hear the echo of his rough growl in my ears.

Fate, that male.

Who was he?

No, I don't want to know.

My pelvic floor squeezes between my legs, remembering how he used me.

Did he seem angry with me? He certainly wasn't pleased.

Perhaps because his life won't accommodate finding a fated mate like mine.

His annoyance didn't stop him from being careful, though. Going slow until I was ready to take his oversized cock.

I loved how rough he was. That alpha dominance I never thought I would enjoy took me to a level of nirvana I've never found before—with or without a partner.

And honestly, before tonight, the best sex I've had was *without* a partner. Just me and my battery-operated boyfriend. But then again, I've only had sex with humans, so maybe that's why.

Tonight, I learned what sex can be. An altered dimension. Alchemy. A place to spar, ignite, and become something completely changed, completely new.

I reach for the door handle and tug.

Oh. Shit.

"No." I smack my palm against the locked door to the school. Even though I know it's locked, I jiggle the door, putting all my strength into it.

Did I actually lock my keys inside my classroom? And my clothes... Oh, fuck.

This couldn't be worse. They're strewn through the hallway of *the high school where I teach.* A high school full of shifters who will know by scent who they belong to! This is...calamitous.

I'm going to lose my job the week after I started. I don't know what got into me. I've never been so overcome by a full moon in my life. I lost all reason.

I turn in a circle, considering my options.

Basically, I don't have any. I can stay here naked and risk being seen by a human–or worse, one of my alpha-hole students—or I can shift and go home.

Fate, if any of those horn-dog ballers who sit in the back of my classroom and ignore me all period saw me right now, I'd forever be the dirty joke of the school. I already know they entertain all kinds of pornographic fantasies about me. Being a young female teacher to a bunch of teen wolves has its hazards.

I suck in a deep breath and let it out slowly.

It's okay. I can manage this. I'll just have to be the first one in the school tomorrow morning. So long as I get here at the same time as the janitor, everything will be fine. Unless the janitor is a horn dog, too.

Fuck. He probably is.

* * *

Lotta

I toss and turn all night, feverish with hormones I haven't felt since I transitioned. I wake in the throes of an orgasm, my fingers between my legs, my sex dripping. I'm arching up off the sheets, my inner thighs shaking where they clamp around my wrist. I don't remember what the dream was. I only know that I still hear the echoes of that male's deep growl in my ears.

I still feel the tremble in every cell in reaction to his voice.

I'm dying to catch his scent again–that leather and spice and manly aroma that hit me like a heady drug.

I sag back on the pillows, trying to catch my breath. Then I look at the clock on my bedside table.

Fuck!

I leap out of bed and bolt for my closet. There's no time for a shower—good thing I took one last night. I'm late. *So* late.

Did I hit snooze in my sleep?

Stupid, stupid, stupid!

How can I be late on the morning when I was supposed to arrive early?

Seriously, what is happening to me? I never oversleep.

Of course, I also never have fever dreams about male wolves making me come out in the wild.

I yank on a T-shirt and skirt without checking to see if they go together. I shove my feet in a pair of flip-flops. Who cares if they are against the district dress code? No flip-flops is a dumb rule, anyway, right along with the sexist rule that girls cannot show bra straps.

In a minute flat, I'm out the door and starting up my Mini Cooper with the spare key I dug out last night after crawling through an open window to the casita where I live.

I step on the gas, screeching the tires as I peel out. It doesn't matter though. While I may arrive before the clang of the first bell, there is no possibility of me being the first or second person in the school. I orgasmed my way right through that chance an hour ago.

I race down the streets and pull into the staff parking lot.

Dear Moon Goddess, get me through this day. I jog into school. I swear everyone's looking at me, but hopefully, it's just paranoia.

I do a quick, surreptitious check, but my clothes are not in the hallway. I'm not sure if that's a good thing or a bad thing, to be honest. I walk to my classroom, where students gather outside my door for the first period. It's a first-year class, one of my easier ones. The younger they are, the easier they are for me to control. My worst class is the sixth-period seniors–the class with Asher Martin, the school football star and leader of the alpha holes.

The neighbor kid who doubled in size since I saw him last and who now absolutely hates me.

I reach for the door to my classroom before I remember I don't have the keys to unlock it.

Dammit. I need to find the janitor or principal.

No, wait. No, no, no. I resist the urge to scurry around like a guilty rat.

I'm a teacher here. I need to maintain my dignity.

I draw up all five-foot-two of my height, puff up my chest, and turn a regal head on the closest student to me. "Andrew, go and find the janitor to unlock my door." I may not be the biggest or strongest wolf in the school, but I am a teacher, and I know how to pull authority.

"Yes, Ms. James."

As soon as he disappears, I wish I'd gone myself.

24

Because now, the seconds stretch out like hours as the bell rings, and I'm still standing in the hallway with my class.

I think fast. "Being an artist means working with what you have where you are," I tell the class. "The bell has rung. Class begins now. Look around this hallway. If you were to depict it in a way that conveyed some meaning, how would you do it?"

No one is listening to me.

I put as much Alpha Command in my voice as I can. "Backs against the lockers."

My students reluctantly shuffle back to form a line against the wall. "Now, let's look at that wall." I point to the wall opposite us. "What do you see, and how would you make a statement about it?"

"What do you mean, *make a statement about it*? It's a wall." One of the female students says, looking at her nails.

"Sure. How many different things can a wall convey?"

Blank stares.

"How do walls make you feel?"

More blank stares.

I offer a little vulnerability. "Sometimes walls make me feel shut in. Imprisoned."

I get some nods as they start to catch my drift.

"So I might paint this wall with an oppressive tilt in my direction as if it were closing in on me. Or how else might I show that?"

"You could paint bars," someone throws out.

"Exactly. I could paint actual prison bars."

"Or you could make the lockers look like prison bars–I know!" –Finally, one of my students gets excited– "You could have the lockers as prison bars and then have them bent open in the middle with a hole to the outside."

"Yeah, and what if everything inside was black and

white, and then the outside could be in full color?" Another student suggests.

I reward her with an encouraging smile. "Now that sounds like an art piece worth making."

The janitor–Zory, I think his name is–arrives with the keys. He doesn't look at me as he unlocks the door and pushes it open for me.

"Thank you, Zory," I murmur.

He grunts in response and walks away without another word.

Someone has been inside the classroom recently. I catch the scent but can't quite identify them. My clothes from last night are folded and neatly stacked behind my desk, underneath my purse.

Okay. I exhale the breath I'd been holding.

Someone had my back.

Maybe nothing is fucked here.

I go with the morning's lesson, telling them that we're going to take a break from their current pointillism project to try some rough sketches of the hallway.

A cheerleader raises her hand.

"Yes, Remi?"

"May I go out in the hallway to sketch?"

I hesitate. I would love to take my class out of the classroom and into the world to start seeing the world through an artist's lens, but I'm not feeling brave enough to buck the system after my behavior last night.

That only compounds when the principal opens the door and leans in. "I need to see you after school."

Fuck.

I'm probably about to be fired. Great. My first professional job lasted all of three weeks. I'm not sure whether Artist Me just self-sabotaged so I won't sell out and stay in

Wolf Ridge, or this is the natural punishment for letting my wolf out.

I don't know. I'm too much of a mess this morning to understand any of my failures or motivations since I arrived.

I swallow. "Yes, sir. I'll be there."

I am so busted.

Chapter Four

Asher

My fingers close into fists as I stride down the hall. My knuckles crack and snap. Eric Damonella is going to die.

At lunch, I heard a rumor–a rumor I am going to kill him for.

Supposedly, he has a pair of Carlotta's panties, and he's saying he came here and hooked up with her during the full moon run last night.

Obviously, I know that's not true.

I know because I still remember the feel of her slender body beneath mine. How it felt to drive into her and make her scream out her pleasure.

He probably brought a pair of his sister's panties to school. All I care about is that he's spreading lies about Carlotta that degrade and objectify her.

I may be the asshole who sits in the back and disrespects her in class, but that sure as fuck doesn't mean I'm going to stand by and let Eric Damonella humiliate her. I have my reasons for hating her.

Reasons she understands. Reasons no one else needs to know.

But I will beat anyone else to a pulp for doing more than following my lead in class.

I throw open the door to the art room. It has one of those hinges that automatically pull it closed, but I hit the door so hard the hinge busts off and clatters to the floor.

I don't give a fuck.

Eric is sitting in the back row, where my buddies and I sit, and he is showing the guys something in the pocket of his backpack.

I drop my backpack and shove a row of tables out of my way as I march through, sending students' artwork flying. Believe it or not, I still don't have Eric's attention. He's too busy telling some fucked up story to Seb and Markley, who I will kill for looking at the pair of panties he's flashing.

"No, dude. I'm not making it up. Smell them for yourself." He balls the fabric in his fist and passes it to Seb.

I nearly lose control of my wolf. I leap over the bank of tables in time to grab Eric's wrist before he completes the pass-off.

Snap.

I break the bones in his wrist with one swift corkscrew spiral.

A human girl in the class screams.

But my wolf isn't satisfied yet.

"Asher Martin!" Lotta snaps, rushing toward us. Her scent enters my nostrils–cool and earthy at once. Jasmine and honey.

She's in a bright turquoise top cropped above her belly button and a plain black skirt that hits above the knee but unfortunately hugs her ass in a way that makes my mouth water.

I glare at that heart shaped perfection. I hate everything about her.

And I don't want her close to me now. Her scent fucks with my wolf, and he's already getting off-leash.

"*Stand down.*"

My wolf recognizes the sound of our mate, but that only riles him further. Like he believes she's in physical danger from this asshole, rather than just reputational.

I palm Eric's head and smash it down on the table, facing Carlotta. "Tell Ms. James what you're saying."

Eric splutters.

"Go on. Tell her." I keep his face pressed to the laminate.

"Let go of me, dude." He struggles to sweep his leg behind mine to take me down.

I pick up my large foot and push it against the side of his knee. "Want me to break the knee, too?"

Eric's a shifter. He'll heal in a couple of days. Still, fights aren't allowed on school property. There are human teachers and students who would be horrified by the level of violence shifters exhibit in a fight. Plus, there will be the problem of explaining why we heal so quickly. Eric will now have to wear a cast, healed or not.

"Dude, what's your problem? I thought you hated Ms. James."

I pick up his head and bash it back down. The human in the front shrieks again. I'm definitely breaking all the pack and school rules right now. There will be hell to pay for this, but I'm used to being the pack pariah. My dad and Lotta made sure of that.

"*Asher!*" Carlotta barks. "That's *enough*. Let him go. *Now.*"

"Apologize to Ms. James." I've cooled down a bit now that he's pinned, and I can smell his pain.

"Sorry, Ms. James," he pants quickly.

"Tell her what you're sorry for." My voice is harder than stone.

I glance at the floor where the panties dropped when he lost control of the use of his fingers. I point. "Give me those," I say to Seb.

Seb complies, picking up the panties and searching my face as he hands them to me. I'm sure my behavior seems like a complete one-eighty. My usual aim in this class is taunting our substitute teacher not defending her.

I hold them up. Everything in me is hardened and mean. "What are you saying about these?"

The part that throws me off is the way Carlotta's face drains of color when she sees the panties.

Are these her panties? Eric *did* tell Seb to smell them.

I shove them in my back pocket, trying to get control of my wolf's rage.

He didn't touch her. No way.

My mind is going wild, though. What if he got to her after I did? No. I don't believe it.

Besides, if he had, she wouldn't have been wearing panties.

So, *what the fuck?*

I turn my attention back to Eric, who I fear I will genuinely murder.

I bang his head once more and punch him in the kidney. "Tell Ms. James what you're saying about her."

"I'm sorry!" Eric yelps. "I said we had sex. I'm an asshole, okay?"

I watch Carlotta's face transform into shock then

31

outrage. But does it mean she didn't have sex with him? Or did she?

Fuck, I'm so off-balance here. I don't know if I can't trust any of my thoughts about that female.

"Both of you, to the principal's office. Now," she snarls.

My gaze meets Carlotta's and locks. Color has returned to her face through two bright spots high on her cheeks. Anger flashes in her golden gaze. "*Now, Asher.*"

I gotta hand it to her. She knows how to infuse alpha command in her tone for such a petite shifter. It doesn't affect me physically, but she sure sounds like she wields deadly force behind it.

I don't want to let go of Eric, but what else can I do? He confessed and apologized. Unless I'm actually going to kill him, the fight is over. Reluctantly, I lift my vise-like hold on his head, then grip him under the armpit to haul him to stand.

I stalk out of the class, grabbing my backpack on the way out the door. Outside the classroom, I turn to give Carlotta another look.

She's watching me with—is it misgiving? Regret?

Well, she should be sorry.

I hope she's spent as many nights awash in misery as my mom and I have for what she did to us.

* * *

Lotta

I tap on Principal Olsen's door even though his secretary told me he was waiting for me.

I'm a teacher now—an adult, I try to remind myself because I'm feeling very much like a naughty school girl. Well, I did fuck up. The adult thing is to own it completely.

Unless he doesn't know what happened. In which case, I should keep my mouth shut. Ack–I don't know how to play this!

"Carlotta." His gaze is disapproving to say the least. "Have a seat."

I sit in the chair opposite him and cross my legs.

"I came in this morning to find your clothing strewn throughout the hallway. Care to explain?"

My face burns hot. Fate, I hope he assumed it was because I shifted and not that I had hot and heavy sex with someone in the school.

"I am so sorry. I had a...mishap last night."

"Of what nature?"

"This is really embarrassing, but the truth is, I haven't shifted since I left for college." I force my hands to stop fidgeting in my lap by holding them tightly together. "After the first few months, I found the full moons actually weakened my energy and life force. But last night while I was painting here, I heard the pack howls, and my wolf awoke. It was like I was a prepubescent teen again–I had no control over the shift. I ran to get out of the school. When I returned, I discovered I'd locked myself out. I planned to come in early to rectify the clothing in the hall situation, but somehow, I guess as a result of my first shift in almost five years, I completely overslept."

I leave out the part about realizing my fated mate is here, in Wolf Ridge. A member of this pack. What are the chances? Of all the hundreds of thousands of wolves scattered across the globe, my fated mate would be from my hometown. The place I am desperate to get out of.

Principal Olsen frowns, exuding that alpha power and sternness that makes him a good principal to a school full of wolf shifters. "You should have contacted me last night when you realized you were locked out."

"Yes, sir." I want to throw out the excuse that my phone was locked inside as well, but I could have gone to my parents' house to borrow one of theirs. I just didn't want to admit to my mom anything of what had transpired.

"You're right. The truth is, I lost control, and then I was embarrassed, and my failure to take responsibility for my actions made it all worse. I'm sorry."

"I'm guessing Eric Damonella found your panties somewhere on campus?"

My face flames hotter. Is it possible to die of humiliation? It's not, right? Because it really seems like I might die right here, right now.

I clear my throat. "Uh, yeah, that's my guess, too."

"I understand he claimed to other students that he had sex with you."

Gross. As if I'd have sex with a student.

Having a kid telling everyone he screwed me was the kind of pervy shit I expected from the situation. What I didn't expect was having Asher Martin defend me.

What was that about?

The guy literally hates me. He sits in the back of my class and mutters backtalk the entire period. I've already given him detention twice for his behavior in my class, and I've only been teaching at Wolf Ridge for two weeks.

Asher never does any of the work I assign. I predict he will be benched soon from playing football because he's failing my class. Which will be a problem, since I understand he's one of the school's star players.

I don't relish delivering that punishment, though. It will just give him another reason to believe I ruined his life.

"I'm sure you know that's not true. That would be highly unethical."

"Yes. I questioned him. He lied about spreading rumors about you, but he told the truth when I asked point-blank if he'd had sexual relations of any kind with you."

I nod.

"I don't want rumors spread about my teachers sleeping with their students in this school. I don't want teacher's panties being handed around by students. If you can't get control of your wolf around the full moon, stay away from this school after hours. I gave you keys and permission to use the art studio on your own time as a favor. Don't make me regret it. Understood?"

"Yes, sir. Perfectly."

I hesitate. Before he dismisses me, I have to ask about Asher.

"Given that it was my folly that caused the fight in my classroom, I hope you, um, didn't go too hard on Asher. He was just...acting gentlemanly, to be honest."

I don't know why that idea makes a knot tighten under my ribs.

Because it shows he cares? No, he clearly doesn't. It just shows there's a decent guy under all that assholery.

"I suspended him for the rest of the week, but allowed him to play in this weekend's game. We have college scouts attending, and he's one of our best."

Relief pours through me. "Good. That's important."

"I will have to notify Alpha Green and the council, though. He broke pack rules showing his nature in front of the humans in your class. Plus, the violence was excessive."

Fuck.

My mom is on that council. She won't be kind to Asher because of her bias against his dad.

My stomach twists. He may be a pain in my ass right now, but I happen to know how much he's been through. If he gets himself banished from the pack, I will be sick over it.

"Are you sure that's necessary?"

I still have this ever-present need to protect Asher. But he's not thirteen anymore. He's eighteen–an adult now. And my past attempt to protect him only messed up his life even more. But somehow, I can't seem to stop myself.

"Are you questioning my judgment?"

"No, sir. Sorry." I stand. "Thank you for your understanding. I won't let it happen again, I assure you."

"See that you don't."

I walk out, trying not to think about Asher's fate. It's his problem, not mine.

It was just my panties that started it. Gah!

Chapter Five

sher

A I wrap my arms around my mom and squeeze her tight. Her thin body trembles against mine, telling me that my fears of being banished from this pack like my dad are founded.

"It's going to be okay," I murmur, not sure if it's true.

We're standing outside the door to Alpha Green's office, where I was summoned by a phone call during dinner.

I've already answered to Principal Olsen, who suspended me from school for the rest of the week.

"If I was being kicked out, this would probably be a council meeting," I whisper.

At least, that's how I think it worked when my dad was banished.

Shame fills my entire being, as it always does when I think of my dad. It was my loose lips that got him banished. I stupidly trusted Lotta James. I confided in her, and she betrayed me.

What a gruesome twist of fate it would be if I was now banished over defending her reputation.

I release my mom and knock lightly on the door.

"Enter."

I step in, and Alpha Green glances at my mom. "Wait outside, Lisa."

She bows her head. "Yes, Alpha."

Alpha Green remains sitting but doesn't indicate that I should sit opposite him, so I remain standing.

"You broke the wrist of a student at school."

"Yes, Alpha."

"At *school.* In front of *humans.*"

"Forgive me, Sir."

He scrutinizes my face.

I work hard to remain perfectly still. Perfectly stoic. I don't allow myself to swallow or sweat. I don't want our pack alpha to smell fear on me. That would confirm the idea that I'd done something wrong.

"Principal Olsen was inclined to forgive your behavior on account of chivalry–you were defending a female teacher."

"He suspended me until Saturday's game, Sir." I point it out in hopes that he'll decide I've already been appropriately punished.

"Eric will have to wear a cast for at least four weeks to avoid suspicion. That's a lot longer than three days, isn't it?"

The fucker deserves it as far as I'm concerned. I keep my face blank of irritation, though. "Yes, sir."

Alpha Green must sense my disagreement because he stands, sending a blast of power in my direction. It's all I can do not to take a step back and show how much it affected me.

"Violence is in your genes, Asher." He points a finger at me. "Your father was violent. This pack put up with incident after incident with him, brushing it off as part of wolf nature, but in retrospect, it's clear he didn't know right from wrong."

I don't know what he's referring to. Sure, my dad got into brawls at the pub. He knocked me and my mom around when he was in a mood. But his ultimate crime wasn't violent.

A familiar mix of shame and anger makes my neck flush with heat. I keep my lips closed, dragging breath in through my nose.

"Do *you*, Asher?"

I blink, not sure what he's asking. My brain was out reviewing this perspective of my dad.

"Do you know the difference between right and wrong?" he roars.

Fuck. I made him mad.

"Yes, Alpha."

He raises his brows. "Do you?"

"Yes, sir."

He glares at me for a moment. "Son, let me explain this very clearly. I won't excuse your violence again. You are a hair's breadth from getting banished like your father. Any more incursions, and you're gone. Understand?"

My heart hammers against my chest. "Yes, sir."

"Dismissed."

I hate this town. I hate this whole damn pack.

I especially hate Lotta James because all of this–this whole damn mess–rests firmly on her slender shoulders.

Lotta

I enter my casita and flop face down on the bed that takes up half the apartment. Sunlight streams in through the windows, making the polished saltillo tile glow like a warm sunset.

I left school after my visit with the principal. I usually stay and paint until late evening, but I'm not capable of doing anything creative right now.

It's a miracle I didn't get fired. I'm not sure how I managed it. Probably only because my mom is pack royalty, and both of my parents are part of Alpha Green's high council.

My phone buzzes with an incoming text.

> What's up, Arizona?

It's from Andy–one of the three human roommates I left behind in Chicago when I realized there was no way I could keep paying rent. We're not friends, but I muddied the waters by playing the *roommates with benefits* game with him for a spell.

What can I say? I was lonely. He was hot, for a human, and available. Too self-involved and just in it for sex to sniff out my secret.

I don't know why he's texting now. We weren't in a more than business texting relationship. Even if that business sometimes included booty calls.

I text back,

> ??

> I'm coming to Scottsdale to meet with a gallery owner my mom knows. I might be able to get you a meeting, too.

Oh. Unexpected. Andy's a trust-funded sculptor. He's never had to work a day in his life. He thinks far too highly of his art and doesn't give a shit about anyone else's. He's not usually the kind of guy to throw anyone a bone.

My pulse picks up speed.

> That would be great. I would appreciate it. Scottsdale is just down the hill from Wolf Ridge.
>
> Cool. I'll let you know.

I'm light-headed. The rumbling in my stomach gets me up off the bed. Something about shifting last night has made me ravenous today. I swear it's like hitting transition again. Great–I'm having a second puberty. As if the first one wasn't awful enough. Coming back here was such a mistake. But what choice did I have?

I failed to find a job in Chicago that paid enough to cover my student loans and rent. I was substitute teaching there for twenty bucks an hour. When the human art teacher at Wolf Ridge High went on medical leave for the rest of the school year, my mom called and talked me into coming home to take the job. The long-term substitute contract pays more than I was making in Chicago. It's a seven-month commitment teaching the subject I love. I decided my mom was right–it's a chance to catch up on my bills and figure out my next move.

Of course, she just wanted me back under her watchful eye. She and my dad could have helped me financially while I was in school–they have plenty of money–but they refused. They were basically starving me out.

Which reminds me, I am starting to shake with hunger. I need protein and not the couple of slices of ham I have in my mini-fridge. I will have to invite myself to dinner with my parents.

They will be delighted. Me, not so much. I walk across the pool deck to their back slider, which I find open. "Hey, guys!"

The house is air conditioned to seventy degrees, and the cool air feels good on my flushed skin. I hadn't realized I was running warm.

"Hi, honey!" My mom has a glass of white wine in her hand, and she's moving around the kitchen, cooking and drinking at the same time. She's still in her work clothes, minus the heels, her sleeveless blouse opened at the throat and coming untucked from her pencil skirt.

"Hey, peanut." My dad is standing on a stepladder, installing new drapes.

My mom gives my outfit a critical up and down. "Tell me you didn't wear those clothes to teach today."

I try to resist my nervous system's instant reaction to her judgment. The heat in my face. The spike of anger. The clench of my palms.

Only seven months.

Then I will move away and pursue my art.

"I woke up late," I confess. I figure if they hadn't already noticed my late departure, someone in this small town is sure to tell them.

"Lotta, I stuck my neck out to get this job for you. Don't embarrass me by proving you're not responsible enough–"

"All right, Denise," my dad cuts in.

"Mom, I know. I'm not blowing off the job. The full moon threw me off."

Both my parents stop what they're doing to peer at me. My mom puts a hand on her hip. "Did you shift?"

Gah. I really don't want to have this conversation with them. They know I didn't shift the entire time I was at college. That I found it easier to fit in and live with humans that way. Of course, that's why they wanted me back home.

"Yes."

They shoot each other pleased looks. "That's great honey," my dad says. "I'll bet it felt good."

I force a smile. "It did. But it ramped up my metabolism. I slept hard, and now I'm starving."

"Well!" My mom beams. "Let's get some food into you. Set the table, hon. I'm almost finished with this beef stir fry."

I hate that they're happy about this. I don't want to admit that my dad was right–it did feel good. The whole situation reeks of a told-you-so. For most of my upbringing, they've been telling me art is for humans. Cities are for humans.

When I chose to attend art school in a big city against their wishes, they told me how bad it was for me to never shift, how I would make myself sick, how my wolf might go dormant, or I might suffer from a human-like ailment like cancer.

They refused to help me with tuition or living expenses in hopes I would tuck tail and return.

For over four years, I've been trying to prove them wrong. So I really hate to make them right about anything. Especially anything that makes them share victorious smiles about me.

I guess that's the trade-off for a home-cooked meal that will actually satisfy my ravenous wolf. I set the table and pour myself a glass of wine, drinking half the glass down in a few gulps to try to relax.

Not that the buzz from alcohol lasts very long for wolf shifters. We metabolize too quickly. Hopefully it will be enough to get through dinner.

My mom finishes and dishes out the meal onto the three plates I set.

I slide into a chair and put my napkin on my lap. My stomach gives a loud rumble.

"Coming," my dad says before my mom tells him. He washes his hands and sits down at the table, searching my face with delight. "I didn't see you on the run last night."

I pick up my fork and dig in. It's a simple dish–snap peas, tomatoes, and beef with cashews and some kind of plum sauce. It tastes like heaven. I gobble down a bite before I answer. "No. I wasn't planning on joining. That's why I didn't go to the pack hall. But I heard the yips and howls from the school and...I guess I couldn't resist." I force a cheerful note into my voice like it was something I chose rather than something my wolf forced onto me.

"Did you find any of your old friends?"

I'm still shoveling food into my mouth. "Uh...I honestly don't know who I was running with." Heat crawls up my neck. I'm suddenly feverish again, remembering that male.

The things he did to me.

Is this what you needed, little wolf?

I haven't been able to stop thinking about him all day. How much I crave his dominant touch again.

Need it.

How I'm afraid to find out who he is. I'd give anything to keep it in the realm of fantasy. A faceless man with an incredible, growly voice who I meet once a month on the full moon run.

Except I'm already dying to see him again. I don't know how I will wait another twenty-seven days.

I even called Dr. Oakley's office at lunch today and made an appointment to get birth control. I'm definitely planning on having sex with this guy again, and I can't risk an unwanted pregnancy. Considering I had no control of myself last night when I was in wolf form, I need to take some precautions.

"But you enjoyed yourself?" my dad presses.

This ass belongs to me. It's mine to do with what I want.

Oh, fate. I'm getting hot and squirmy right here at my parents' dinner table. I shove another giant bite of food into my mouth and chew, nodding. "Uh huh."

I don't realize for a moment that my mom has stopped eating to stare at me.

I force myself to slow down. Purposely set down my fork.

"You *were* hungry, weren't you?"

I pick up my wine glass and drain it. "Unexpectedly so. Sorry to come over here and barge in on your dinner, but I couldn't even wait to fix myself something."

"No, we're delighted to have you any time, darling. I wonder if you'll fill out a bit now that you're shifting again."

Ugh. Now the body shaming stuff. My mom seriously drives me nuts. I work on cleaning my plate.

"You might have just been a late bloomer, and that's why you were able to suppress your wolf while you were at college. I want you to go and see Dr. Oakley for a full checkup."

"I already called for an appointment," I cut her off.

"She's an adult now, Denise," my dad chides. "She's been on her own for years now."

"I know, I know." My mom holds up her hand in his direction without taking her eagle eye from me. "Why did you make an appointment?"

I stare right back at her. "Birth control."

"Oh!" That shocks her into a moment of silence. "Well that's great. Does that mean you really *did* enjoy that full moon run?" She waggles her brows. Of course, she'd love it if I found someone here who would make me stick around.

"Ugh." I stand, taking my cleaned plate with me. "Enough, Mom. Respect my boundaries, please." I rinse my plate and set it in the dishwasher.

My mom has enough grace to laugh. "All right, honey. I'm sorry. I just care about you, that's all."

Oh, I know. She just cares about me in an interfering, overbearing way.

I lean over and kiss her cheek. "Thanks for dinner, Mom." I kiss my dad's cheek, too. "Love you both. Bye!"

I cruise out the door before they can grill me anymore.

I'm seriously ready for a second meal. Like that one gave me enough energy to get in my car and drive to In 'n Out burger for more protein.

That's what I'll do. Get a second meal and go back to the school to paint.

Hopefully, I won't wolf-out again and lose my panties to another idiot student.

Chapter Six

sher

"Three-day suspension from school, but I still get to play in Saturday's game," I report to Abe when he stops by the bakery after practice. I'm pretty sure me playing is against District policy, but football is king in Wolf Ridge. The fact that I'm the star of our defense is probably the only reason I didn't get a harsher punishment.

"Good. Is that all?"

We're in the back warehouse where my mom sent me to clean and organize Mrs. Angelson's supplies. It's my punishment for being suspended from school.

Not that helping Mrs. Angelson is ever a punishment. The old she-wolf is like a grandmother to me. She's been my mom's employer since I was a pup, so Wolf Ridge Sweet Treats is my second home. I've been working weekends for her since I was fifteen.

Before I hit puberty and got on the football team, I used to come here every day after school until closing time. Mrs. Angelson would have a warm peanut butter and chocolate chip cookie and a glass of milk waiting for me to take to the corner table where I'd do my homework.

That same table where Carlotta tutored me in math, driving me insane with her jasmine and honey scent. The way she'd tug and twist on that golden moon pendant while she watched me work out a problem.

"No. Alpha Green said one more strike and I'm out." That's the part I'm trying not to think about.

I could be thrown out of the pack before I finish high school. Any hope I had—slim though it is—of getting a college scholarship for football would be demolished.

"Fuck." Abe starts picking up fifty pound bags of flour and tossing them to me, so I can stack them neatly in large plastic tubs with lids. The warehouse sits behind the quaint main-street bakery. In the early 1900's, it was a small flour mill until competition with the larger Hayden Mill in Tempe shut it down. Now, it's a large, empty brick building that Mrs. Angelson uses to store extra supplies.

"So what happened? Seb and Markley said you lost it."

I shrug. "Damonella pissed me off."

"I heard he had Carlotta James' panties."

My upper lip curls, but I manage to keep my growl choked down.

"So you taught him a lesson in manners?"

I throw the bag of flour so hard it splits when it hits the wall, sending a giant cloud of whole wheat flour into the air. Dammit. A ripped bag was the whole reason Mrs. Angelson had me in here cleaning to begin with. She wants everything spic and span, so rodents can't get to anything.

"Dammit," I mutter. Now I'll owe her the cost of the flour.

"So you were defending the honor of a female teacher. That's a legit defense. I don't see what the problem is."

I grunt in reply. "The problem is everyone in this town thinks I'm destined to be trouble like my dad."

"What is it with you and Ms. James?" Abe tosses me another bag.

I catch it but throw it back. "Hold up. I have to move all these to sweep up the mess again." I shove the bins in his direction to empty the stack against the wall.

"You dodging that question?" Abe leans against the wall, arms folded over his chest.

I consider telling him the truth. I mean, Abe just marked a human. And he's been dealing with some kind of seizure thing that he hid from us for who knows how long. It's not like Dr. Oakley's perfect son is actually perfect.

"You had the hots for her when we were in middle school. I mean, we all did. She's cute as fuck. But I know her mom was responsible for getting your dad kicked out of the pack."

I shake my head. "*She* was. Lotta–" I cut myself off, the bitter taste of betrayal making my tongue thick. I hate this story so much. I've never told anyone–not even my mom, and I don't want to start now.

Abe watches me with curiosity.

Fuck it. I'm going to tell him. "Can you keep a secret?"

He steps closer, dropping that habitual smirk of his. "You know I can, man."

"She was *directly* responsible."

"Yeah?"

I nod. "Yeah. I told her–I don't fucking know why–that my dad was stealing from the brewery. I told her in confidence. She swore to me she wouldn't tell."

"But she did?"

I nod. "She sure as hell did. It was her mom who got him kicked out."

"Shit." Abe shoves his fingers through his hair. "It's not your fault, man."

I suddenly feel like the wind got knocked out of me. To have Abe understand the level of guilt I feel for being responsible opens a wound I haven't even examined myself. I locked that shit up tight at the time. Too ashamed to tell my mom what I'd done. To admit it's my fault she became a single mom five years ago.

"There's more." I got that off my chest, I might as well tell him everything.

"What?"

"Fate fucked me." I lift my brows and leave that dangling in the air, waiting for Abe to understand.

It takes a moment, and then his eyes widen. "Are you saying–"

I nod.

"She's your mate? Fuck. That's harsh. So harsh, man. I'm sorry. Does she... I mean, have you guys–"

"She doesn't know." I leave out the part about us hooking up last night. I'm not a kiss and tell kind of guy. Plus my wolf is insanely protective of Lotta despite my hatred for her.

I see sympathy in Abe's gaze, which pisses me off. It's the same sympathy I got from my friends after Alpha Green threw my dad out of the pack and the rest of the town shunned me and my mom.

I grab the last sack of flour, my upper lip curling in a snarl, but before I can front, Abe surprises me. "Can you keep a secret for me?"

My brows pop. "Course." I shovel the lost flour from the floor with the dustpan, dumping it into the trash.

"Lauren's not all human."

I stop and stare at him. "What?"

He tosses me the broom. "She's part bear. We think her grandfather might be that old bear that was hanging out on pack land last month."

I whistle. "No shit. So that's why fate put you with her." I start to sweep up the remaining flour.

Abe nods. "So maybe there's a reason, you know?" He shrugs. "I tried to resist her, but it just drove my wolf nuts."

I work the corner with the broom, trying to get it all up. "You think there's a reason Fate chose Carlotta for me?" I shake my head. "No way. I mean, she's hot as fuck, so in theory, we'd make cute pups, but that won't happen."

"That's what I thought, too."

"Nope." I won't let it happen. "I'd choose moon madness if it came to that over marking that female."

Abe leans against the back wall and folds his arms over his chest. "That could be your defense. For the council, I mean. The fact that she's your mate. No one is going to fault you for defending your fated mate's reputation."

I sit on the stack of flour sacks. "I know. But I'm not going to tell the whole fucking town before—"

I stop. Before what? Before I tell Lotta?

Is that what I plan to do?

I haven't even figured out my next move beyond hunting her down again at the next full moon run.

Somehow, I doubt I'll make it that long, though.

The need to get my hands on her grows every minute of the day.

"Before you mark her?"

"I'm not going to mark her," I snarl. But I know it's a lie.

I'm going to sink my teeth into that delectable flesh of hers and leave my scent, so no other male ever touches her.

That doesn't mean I'll keep her.

It will be a catch and release situation.

Except I know that's a lie, too.

I'm going to mark Lotta, and then I'm going to tie her to my bed and punish her in every delicious way possible for the misery she's caused me.

I just have to graduate high school first, so I don't create a scandal even bigger than the one that got my dad thrown out of town.

* * *

Lotta

"You're an asshole for not coming back, even for a visit," my high school friend, Olive declares, narrowing her long, fake lashes at me.

"Seriously," Brianna agrees. We're at the New Moon Diner where the two arranged to meet me, so we could catch up.

"I know. I'm sorry. It's just...it was hard to live with humans, so I kind of needed to cut off my old life, so I could adapt."

There are two paths for Wolf Ridge pack members after high school–death or rebirth. That's my take on it, anyway. Death is staying. You'll work at the brewery or some other local business, get knocked up by another pack member, and dig in to die here the way everyone in your lineage has. Or, if you're lucky and work hard enough, you can get out. But it will mean living away from the pack amongst humans, which has its stressors. In order to survive, you'll have to be reborn as a human.

"It's good to see you. I didn't even realize how much I missed your faces."

I'm lucky they aren't more pissed at me, considering I didn't even attempt to call anyone even after I arrived here two weeks ago. I bumped into Olive at the grocery store last week and guiltily asked who else from our circle was around. She called Brianna, and here we are.

They both were cheerleaders for Wolf Ridge–incredible gymnasts who built sky-high pyramids and tossed each other twenty feet in the air. Now, they are stuck in Wolf Ridge. Brianna works in the nail salon. Olive has a job at an upscale clothing boutique down the mountain in the wealthy human community, Cave Hills.

"Yeah. I heard Wilde Woodward is struggling playing football at Duke. He purposely got into some kind of trouble to get kicked off the team, but he's back there now to finish out the season, at least."

"Duke, wow. That's impressive." I'm out of loop on all the news. Sure, my mom still called me while I was at school and talked my ear off about the pack news, but I think I missed hearing someone made it out of here to *Duke*.

I wonder, briefly, if Asher is good enough to get a scholarship somewhere. But he hates school, so I doubt he'd want to go on. From what I can tell, the work I put into raising his math and writing literacy when I tutored him went down the tubes after his dad got banished.

My stomach tightens into a familiar knot at that thought. You'd think after four and a half years, I would've forgiven myself, even if there's no chance of Asher ever forgiving me.

"What do you think it takes to get nailed by Coach Jamison?" Olive murmurs, stirring her milkshake with her straw and ogling the gorgeous thirty-something high school football coach.

He's sitting a few booths over. With shifter hearing, he probably heard her, if he's bothering to listen.

I force myself to slow down sipping my espresso milkshake. I nearly drained the whole thing the moment Sandra, our waitress—another girl who never made it out of Wolf Ridge—set it down in front of me. Fate, my appetite has been out of control since the full moon. This meal is going to cost more than I wanted to spend.

"Who does he fuck during full moon runs?" Brianna wonders aloud.

My inner thighs slap together at the mention of the full moon. I'm still spending far too many thoughts on who my mysterious lover was and the things he did to me.

"He doesn't. Or if he does, he's discreet."

"He'd have to be careful. He's supposed to be a role model to all his players. He's the one providing them with all the straight talk about sex and she-wolves," I say.

What if...*he* was my full moon romp? Heat crawls across my chest. Maybe my lover isn't already in a relationship. Maybe he didn't show himself because he's an important figure in the pack and has to be careful about gossip. I find myself looking over at his booth, too.

"I'm going to follow him next month," Olive declares.

"Do you know what his wolf looks like?" I try to make the question sound off-hand.

"Doesn't everyone? He's a huge grey."

Grey. Not black. Not my mate.

Brianna turns her dark-eyed gaze on me. "So? Did you have a human boy-toy in Chicago?"

I flush and put my lips around my straw to stall. "I had a roommate with benefits, but I ended it when it got old."

"Ooh, was it awkward?"

I shake my head. "No. This guy's ego was so big, I don't think he even understood he got dumped. He was still trying to get with me every night he was home until I moved out."

Brianna wrinkles her nose. "Ew. Did you kick him in the nuts?"

"Nah. It was annoying, but not dangerous. I had other things to worry about–like finding a job that covered rent."

Olive gives me a sympathetic look. "Did it suck there? I think it would be impossible to live in a city." She reaches across the table and squeezes my hand. "We're so glad you're back."

"Yeah...thanks." My voice sounds hollow.

Brianna doesn't miss it. "You don't want to be back, do you?"

I wince. "Not really. The art scene here is non-existent."

"What about Scottsdale?" Olive asks. "It's just down the mountain. They have tons of art galleries there. You should take your stuff and see if they'll show it."

"Yeah, but you need to know someone to make that happen. You know, be a part of the scene. My former room-mate might have a connection for me, but I haven't heard back yet." I watch myself as I throw up roadblocks. Why am I so afraid? Why don't I follow up with Andy? I try to shake off my resistance. "But that's a good idea. I should try anyway. You never know what might happen."

"I'll go with you if you need moral support," Olive offers.

My lips fall open in surprise. "You would? Really?" Fate, I'm so used to thinking no one in this town supports my art, her offer comes as a shock. Especially considering what a shitty friend I've been.

She shrugs. "Sure. I know how to deal with snobby humans. It's what I do all day at work."

My vision goes wavy for a moment, and I hold my

breath until it passes. "Amazing." I bob my head. "That would be absolutely amazing. Thank you."

"Girl, that's what friends are for. Pack sticks together."

Pack sticks together.

That statement tumbles around like a square peg that can't find its hole. I'm *not* sticking with this pack. I'm going back to the human world where I can flourish as an artist. And yet, this taste of support and camaraderie I've been missing makes me feel like I can inhale a full breath for the first time in years.

I may only be here for a few months, but I don't have to push away friendship to survive anymore. I lean forward and snatch one of Brianna's fries. "So, wait until I tell you what happened to me on the full moon!"

Chapter Seven

Lotta

I shiver against the breeze. In the desert, the temperature drops significantly at night, and I'm still in my shorts and midriff top.

I'm sketching under the soft glow of the Christmas lights I strung up under the roof of my back patio. The front patio of the studio casita my parents rent to me faces the pool and their house which is why I prefer this side. Here I have some privacy. I face the wilderness which inspires the backdrop of my sketch.

In the foreground is a giant she-wolf. It's not me. This one is an alpha wolf. I see her in my dreams. She's white like the snow. Sleek. Powerful.

I set the charcoal and sketchpad down and wrap my arms around myself as I stare into the darkness.

Tonight the wild is calling to me.

Shift. Change. Run.

Find your mate.

Perhaps it's not the wild. Maybe it's just my wolf itching to be free again.

I haven't been the same since the full moon run. It's been impossible to sleep. I lie awake, feverish and full of energy. When I do sleep, my dreams are haunted by *him*.

My wolf wants her mate. She wants another round with him. Wants me to figure out who he is. Where to find him. How to get his attention.

I wake every morning sweaty, horned up, and desperate for a release.

I turn my head, listening to what sounded like a soft footfall.

But no. I'm imagining things. All I hear is the sound of car horns blaring in celebration. The Wolf Ridge football team must've won their game. Earlier cheers drifted on the breeze from the stadium. The team always puts on a great show for the town.

I didn't go to the game, despite my wolf's desperation to get out there and sniff every man in town. There's something about being home when the rest of the town is gathered that feels juicy. Probably because those were the only times I could focus on my art when I lived under my parents' rule.

I wonder whether Asher was allowed to play in tonight's game. He was absent from class for the last three days, but football matters here. I wouldn't be surprised if Principal Olsen let him on the field tonight. He would consider Asher's actions in my classroom justified from a wolf perspective. A male wolf defending the honor of a female is part of our culture. It's just that those actions aren't allowed at school or in front of humans.

I sigh and stand from the patio chair. I'm too restless to enjoy the beautiful night. My skin is hot and itchy. Maybe I should just shift and try to run it off. Would I sleep better? Or would it compound my problems?

I turn toward the door and freeze. The gasp is so sharp it hurts my throat.

If this were a horror film, they would have played that jump-scare sound. You know, the angry violin slash?

Because standing on my porch is the hulking form of one of my students.

Not just any of my students. The one who hates me because of a judgment call I made five years ago. The one I just had suspended for fighting in my classroom.

Asher Martin.

His eyes narrow as he lifts his nose to take in my scent. "You're afraid of me." Is that scorn in his voice?

It seems more like anger.

But maybe that's just his everyday vibe toward me.

Hell, it was his general vibe even before he hit full puberty and became a wolf. He grew up in a violent home. Violence breeds violence, as we all know.

And right now, I have a 250-pound angry linebacker standing on my porch, no doubt here for revenge. Whether it's revenge for the past or revenge for getting him suspended this week, I can't be sure.

I glance toward my parents' house. Should I call for help? They might be back from the game by now. But then there would be more repercussions for Asher. My mom would have him punished to the full extent of pack law for threatening me. I'm not sure I want that for him. I never believed he deserved the angry rebel hoodlum reputation he got in this town.

Asher's nostrils flare when I look toward the house. "Thinking of calling for help?" He prowls closer.

I hold my ground with my neck stiff and straight, but my heart hammers against my sternum. My palms are damp with sweat. I know Asher smells my fear.

"You really don't understand why I'm here, do you, Lotta?" His voice is soft and dangerous. He drops the *Ms. James*, which is just as well. He always manages to infuse it with enough taunt to make me certain it doesn't convey any respect.

"You think I want revenge. That makes sense after what you did to me and my family." He steps even closer.

I resist the urge to back up. I'm still Asher's teacher, dammit.

"Or maybe you think I want something from you." He cocks his head, studying me. "Maybe I'm here to see if you're really taking off your panties for your students."

A flash of anger brings out my wolf, but it's too late.

Asher moves before I finish balling my fists. He pins me up against the wall of the casita with a hand around my throat, his other hand holding under one knee.

I cry out with shock at his sudden violence. But I realize he isn't choking me. I'm dangling above the ground, my weight held by my knee rather than my throat.

He's just scaring me. Showing me how much stronger he is. What he's capable of. One squeeze of that powerful fist, and he could snap my neck. No amount of shifter healing properties would bring me back from that.

"Let's see if you can figure out the real reason I'm here," he growls.

I try to kick him in the balls, but he traps my free leg by pinning it against the wall with his hips. His body presses against mine. I feel every ridge of his rock-hard muscles.

I'm sweating and cold at the same time.

"Close your eyes, Lotta." His growl is a low rumble now.

I stare at him in confusion. What?

"Close them and take a deep breath. Then tell me why I'm here."

I don't move. I'm still holding my breath, trying to decipher what in the hell he's saying. What does he want from me?

"Breathe." There's Alpha Command in his voice, and my body instinctively responds.

I suck in a deep breath, searching his face for a clue.

"Close your eyes." Alpha command again.

My lids snap closed. The heat of his breath whispers across my face. His forehead touches mine.

"Why am I here, Carlotta?" The growl is low now. Taunting.

With my eyes closed, my other senses sharpen. I hear the pounding of my own heart. The wheeze of my breath. The scent of my fear mingled with the deeper notes of hi–

Oh!

My eyes fly open.

Leather and spice.

Oh no.

No, no, no.

It can't be.

Asher Martin *cannot* be my lover from the full moon run.

Oh. Fuck.

I thought it was an older man. Someone who couldn't claim me because he already had a mate. Not a student.

But there's no denying his scent nor my body's response to it.

Fate sent me an impossible match. Fate is seriously fucking with me.

Because Asher Martin–one of my students and a bitter enemy–cannot be my mate.

As soon as I figure it out, Asher releases me, and my feet drop softly to the floor. He stares down at me with a considering look. "So."

Damn him. How dare he fuck with me like that? He didn't allow me to see his identity because he knew it wasn't right. That I never would've consented to having sex with him. He put my job in peril.

I slap him across the face. It's challenging because he's so much taller than I am. The slap stings my hand and seems to have zero effect on him. I slap again, harder. Then, a third time. Still zero effect. I crank my arm back to hit him a fourth time, but he grabs my wrist and spins me around, pinning it to my waist, with my back yanked up against his front. "Slap me again, and I will spank your ass pink," he growls in my ear.

Fate, help me. Heat blooms between my legs and suffuses my neck and face. All I can think about is that spanking he gave me out in the woods. How wonderful it felt to be mastered by his strong, commanding body. How much I want him to repeat it.

No. Fate, no. This is wrong on every level.

Asher releases me, and I immediately bolt, my hand reaching for the door handle to the casita. I throw open the door and rush inside, but he's right behind me. He picks me up and tosses me onto the center of the bed. He's just showing off his physical dominance now. Making sure I remember how big and strong he is and how small I am.

I scramble to my feet, standing on the bed where I can tower over him for a change, like a little dog standing on a chair to bark at a bigger one.

Of course, Asher is not intimidated by me in the slightest.

"So." He advances to the edge of the bed. "I will tell you

why I came here." He reaches into his pocket and pulls out my panties.

Damn him. Of course he has them.

Why didn't it occur to me to demand them back after the fight?

He holds up the slip of red silk dangling from his thumb. I try to snatch them away, but he lifts his hand out of my reach. "I want to know why the fuck Eric Damonella had my mate's panties."

"I'm not your mate!" I blurt even though it's so obviously not true. What I mean is I didn't consent to be his mate. I'm not going to let him claim me. This isn't happening. Even if we weren't complete enemies, he's my student and five years younger. It's an impossibility.

He arches one brow. Which I, unfortunately, find incredibly sexy.

Wait. No.

I can't be attracted to this guy. *He's a boy.*

Except nothing about Asher Martin is boyish. He's six feet five inches tall, two hundred fifty pounds of solid muscle, and eighteen years old. Asher is *all man* now. Alpha wolf. The looks that were heartbreakingly beautiful on him when he was still a scrawny thirteen-year-old now make him drop-dead gorgeous.

"You know that's not true."

He waves the panties. "Tell me he didn't touch you, so I know I'm not committing murder tonight."

Chapter Eight

Asher

Lotta puts her hands on her hips and glares down at me. "It's none of your business."

I bare my teeth. "Tell that to my wolf." A deadly strain to my voice makes the hairs on her arms stand up.

She has to know wolf will want blood. I couldn't help himself from attacking Eric in her classroom last week for disrespecting her. I may hate her, but my wolf will defend her to the death. It's just simple shifter biology.

I shove the panties into my back pocket and grip one of Lotta's slender ankles. One quick tug, and she's off balance, falling backward. I throw a hand out to cradle her head, softening her landing on the mattress.

Her eyes are wild. Her jasmine and honey scent is all over the place–a mixture of fear, anger, and lust.

Being near her simultaneously soothes and riles my wolf. I want her so fucking bad; it's hard not to claim her right here, right now.

Of course, that can't happen. Even if she didn't hate me, I don't want her.

I can't trust her. Her family hates mine.

Lotta's slender form is centered on her king-sized bed, which takes up most of the studio apartment. A pristine white eyelet bedspread frames her, and the heap of fluffy pillows by the headboard make it look like she's a stunning model posing in an interior design magazine.

She rises to her elbows, her cheeks flushed with color. There's a green glow to her eyes. Her wolf is showing. Whether it's from danger or desire, I can't be sure.

The desire to shred that bedding, break the headboard, and find out exactly why a tiny she-wolf like Lotta needs such a giant bed overwhelms me.

So does the need to know about the panties.

"Tell me he didn't touch you," I growl. I don't mean to put a threat in my tone. Or rather, the threat is meant for Eric, not her, but her throat bobs.

"He didn't touch me."

My wolf is so fucking pleased with her answer. Not just because he didn't touch her–I didn't really believe he had– but because she offered up the answer. She's agreeing it *is* my business.

I manacle both her ankles with my hands. "How did he get the panties?"

Lotta's gaze flicks to my touch, and she tugs one ankle back, testing my grip, but the scent of her arousal blooms in the room.

She wants me. We may be completely at odds with one another, but the biology is there. There's no one for her but me.

No one for me but her.

I drag her ankles closer. Her knees are bent, so her butt comes toward the edge of the bed. "Tell me, Lotta."

"I hadn't shifted since I went to college," she says.

My brows rise in shock. I want to grill her about that, but I don't stop her story.

"I didn't plan on shifting for the full moon. I was at school, painting. I heard the pack, and then it was like I was a teenager in transition. I was starting to shift before I even knew it was happening. I stripped out of my clothes as I ran for the back doors. I'm lucky I didn't shred my clothes. When I came back, I realized I was locked out of the school. My phone and my keys were inside. I meant to come in early the next morning, but I slept like I was in transition, too. Principal Olsen picked up my clothes, but he must've missed the panties."

I can't control the low growl issuing from my throat. The thought of any male–principal or student–touching her panties makes me want to bash in the windows of the school and set the whole place on fire.

It must frighten her because Lotta tries to pull out of my grasp, straining to kick me.

I pin her feet to the bed, sliding them wider, so her knees fall open. My wolf is right at the surface. I know my eyes must be glowing. The desire to possess her, to make sure no other male ever spreads a rumor about her again makes my brain short-circuit.

All I can think about is sex.

Domination.

Doing dirty, disrespectful things to that hot little body of hers. More disrespectful even than last time.

"How do I punish my mate for giving another male her panties?" I don't mean it. At least, I didn't even think of the words before they came from my mouth. But the moment I say them, my dick goes harder than steel. The idea of spanking that pretty ass of hers causes a fizzy excitement to shoot through my veins. I remember how much she liked it last time.

Remember how excited she got when I threatened it on her porch tonight.

In the state of my arousal, I fail to notice that she's not excited this time. She's too intimidated. She attempts to kick me again. "I didn't give them to him! For fates' sake, Asher I just told you what happened."

My palms shift to her knees, and I push them wider, up toward her shoulders.

Lotta's breath shudders in her belly as she pants, staring at me. Her eyes are bright green, showing her wolf.

I lean forward, drawn to the delicate flesh of her inner thigh. I nip her there, then drag my open mouth along the soft, sweet skin, licking and biting as I advance toward the apex of her thighs.

The scent of her arousal cloaks my head. I open my mouth wide and cover her entire crotch. Her thin shorts are no barrier to the heat and damp I feel through them. I scrape my teeth along her sex.

"Wh-what are you doing?"

What *am* I doing?

I have no right to be here between Carlotta James's thighs. She didn't invite me. She didn't consent. And she already slapped me three times for taking from her without consent last time.

Just because I'm her mate doesn't mean I can overpower her and take what I want.

It should be the opposite. I should respect her. Treat her like a fucking queen. So what am I doing here?

I release her knees. Her feet drop down to the bedspread.

She's still breathing hard, sucking her breath in and out like she's just run a race.

I straighten, holding her gaze. I'm sure my wolf is showing in my eyes, like hers. But we are at odds with each other. This is a forbidden match. I may be a consenting adult, but she's a teacher at Wolf Ridge. I'm a student. Besides, she doesn't want me. I certainly don't want her. As I back up to the door, our gazes remain locked.

"Asher."

No. I don't want to have this discussion with her. I don't want to hear anything she has to say.

I wrench the door open and go through, slamming it on the way out. I jog into the desert, down to the wash that links the townhouses where I live with my mom with Carlotta's parents' upscale property.

I stop and lean against the shadowy side of our building.

My wolf is all riled up. He wanted Carlotta. He's pissed I left.

"You can't force a loveless mating," I mutter aloud, trying to soothe the aggression before I do something stupid. Something that gets me in trouble once again.

Seems like I'm always in the fucking doghouse in this stupid town.

Carlotta's jasmine and honey scent still lingers in my nostrils. The taste of her skin is still on my tongue. It will be impossible for me to sleep tonight.

Remembering I still have a piece of her with me, I pull her panties out of my back pocket and inhale deeply.

I hear the bang of a screen door as someone steps out into their tiny plot of property.

The flick of a lighter tells me it's Murph Downy, a lineworker at the brewery. "Hey," he barks. "What are you doing out here?"

And there it is.

More trouble.

"Nothing. Just going home." I shove the panties back in my pocket and head toward our townhouse.

"Aren't you Johnny Martin's kid?"

Right. Because everyone in this fucking town thinks I'm cut from the same cloth as my dad.

Fuck this. I square off to him, showing him my full size and a sliver of aggression to prove that I'm not going to back down because he's older. I'm fucking bigger. This asshole isn't going to bully me because of some assumption he's made based on my last name. "So?"

He narrows his eyes and looks me up and down, then spits into the bushes.

"So, I'm watching you, kid."

I bite back the *fuck off* that comes to my lips. That would be going too far. "Watch all you want," I mutter, stalking away, into my own mini yard.

* * *

Lotta

I lie on the bed, panting. My body is feverish. The flesh between my legs is swollen, pressing against the seam of my shorts. It's beyond achey. It's painful.

Asher just did the worst possible thing.

Not the part where he threw me on the bed and spread my legs without my permission. Not the part where he nipped and licked up my thigh. Not even when he put his hot mouth right over the seam of my shorts and bit down like he was taking a bite of peach.

Even though for a minute there, I thought it was going to get rapey.

Just like out on the full moon run, I wasn't sure if I would have a choice or not. I wasn't sure whether I wanted to be given one.

There's something so thrilling about being under a male who could snap my neck with one twist of his big hand.

But the worst thing was when he walked away, straight out my door and into the night.

He walked away without satisfying me. Without taking off my shorts and putting his tongue where I desperately wanted it. Without climbing up on my bed and getting rough with me in a way that forces my surrender. Without giving me that punishment he promised.

And I didn't know until he left how badly my body craves Asher's touch. I need it as much as I need to breathe.

I get up off the bed, my legs wobbly. I go into the bathroom and splash water over my flushed face. My wolf eyes look back at me in the mirror. I'm still itchy and hot. I can't think straight. Why did he leave without finishing what he started?

Was that the punishment? Leaving me aroused and needy and completely unsatisfied? I had no idea this was what it means to be near your mate.

Or was Asher showing mercy because he thought I didn't want it? I probably looked like I didn't. Did I tell him *no*? I can't remember now. I was nervous, for sure.

I was downright afraid when he first showed up, and that made him angry. He needed me to understand why he was here. He may hate me, but he's my mate. He can't stay away from me any more than I can refuse him when he shows up.

We're biologically wired for each other, as horrible as that may be for both us.

Ugh!

Still shaky and hot, I strip out of my clothes and turn on the shower to cold. Maybe if I wash his scent off me, I'll be able to calm down.

Fate, I hope so, or the chances of me sleeping tonight are nil.

Chapter Nine

sher

AI don't sleep a minute all night or the next. I just lie awake, tossing and turning. Jacking off over and over again to try to stop myself from shifting and running the short distance back to Lotta's casita.

Fates, I suddenly understand the human lore about werewolves–the idea of a shifter chaining himself up, so he won't shift and go out.

That's what I need to do. Because I'm quite certain if I let myself shift, I would smash Lotta's door down and claim that female so hard the entire town of Wolf Ridge would hear her screams.

Monday morning, I find myself out of bed before dawn. I yank open the top drawer to my dresser and shove aside my socks. I pick up the last envelope that arrived addressed to me in my dad's handwriting. It came about six months ago. Inside, there was no note. Just nine crisp one hundred dollar bills wrapped in a torn piece of notebook paper with scratches that look a lot like bets on them.

He's probably cage fighting. Or stealing again—who knows.

The last envelope came eight months before this one. There's no rhyme or reason to when they come or how much he sends. He's never sent a letter with it. But he never was the kind of dad to say anything nice.

I guess I should be grateful he remembers he has a son.

Even before my dad got kicked out, he wasn't much of a father figure. Now, because my mom refused to leave with him when he was banished, he's completely out of touch. He doesn't call or text or Facetime. We have no idea where he lives or what he does.

My mom refuses to take any of the money—she's too pissed at my dad for what he did. She says the cash is probably dirty, and it's for me anyway—his form of child support—so I can do what I want with it. I try to stretch it as long as I can, chipping in to buy us groceries, pay my own expenses, and buy my mom nice birthday and Solstice presents.

I crack the envelope open now. There are three hundreds left. I don't know why I'm looking. Why my thoughts are connecting money to Lotta. Like I'm going to use it to court her. Or show off to her. Or provide for her.

As if.

Beneath the envelope is a slender chain with a thin crescent moon pendant made of real gold.

I pick it up now and bring it to my nostrils as if it might still hold Lotta's scent after all these years. It doesn't, but it helps me conjure that sweetness, anyway. Jasmine, honey, and the mouth-watering scent of her feminine arousal make my head swim.

I give it a rough shake.

I shower and get on my motorcycle, beating my mom to Wolf Ridge Sweet Treats. The scent of freshly baked croissants fill the alleyway where I park my motorcycle. Mrs. Angelson is already working inside, unwrapping a stick of butter to throw in the churning mixer.

Her wrinkled face lights up with a smile when I come in the back door. The rest of the town may think I'm a hoodlum, but Mrs. Angelson has always treated me like I was special. In fact, if she hadn't stood behind my mom when my dad got kicked out of the pack, I'm not sure my mom and I would have even been able to stay in Wolf Ridge. She found extra hours to give my mom after my dad left even when she didn't need the help. Even when making ends meet was a strain for her, too.

"Good morning, Asher. You're up early. I thought your suspension was over today."

I lean down and press my cheek to her wrinkled one to give her a kiss. "It is. But I came to take care of your morning deliveries."

"Aren't you sweet? They haven't come yet. Why don't you get the coffee urn filled with water." She points to the three-compartment sink where the urn has been filling with filtered water. I pick it up and carry it to the front of the bakery where I plug it in and add the fresh coffee grounds. I turn it on to brew, so people can self-serve when they come in for their morning pastry.

My mom unlocks the front door and stares at me in surprise. "Asher! I thought you were still home in bed. What are you doing here? You have school today, you know.
"

"I couldn't sleep. I came to see if I could be of use."

My mom's concerned face softens into affection. "You are a sweet boy."

"You're the only person on this planet who thinks I'm sweet," I say with a grin.

Not true," Mrs. Angelson calls from the back.

"All right, the two of you, then." I walk into the kitchen, pick up a chocolate croissant from the tray she just pulled out of the oven, and take a giant bite. "Mmm. Delicious."

Mrs. Angelson pokes me. "You just came here for breakfast, didn't you?"

"Mmm. It's absolutely perfect, Mrs. A." The flaky pastry melts in my mouth, dark chocolate oozing over my tongue.

My mom comes into the kitchen and puts an apron on. She falls into work beside Mrs. A without being told what to do. "I can see it going either way with you," she says, picking up the dropped thread of conversation.

"Oh, boy," I mutter. She lectured me all weekend about the fight at school, and it seems she's not done yet.

My mom doesn't know I'm in a class taught by our nemesis Carlotta James. Which means she also doesn't know she was the teacher responsible for getting me suspended. If she knew, should be even more upset, and I don't like to upset my mom. She went through four years of depression after my dad left, even though he wasn't a fated mate, and she's barely recovered from it now.

"You have the capacity to be an alpha, but you won't get your shot at leadership if you don't straighten up, Asher. You can't go around breaking wrists and smashing noses at school and expect anyone to think you're alpha material. It takes more than big muscles and a deep growl to command respect. In fact, your size may work against you when it comes to this town. People are afraid of a big wolf who carries bitterness in his heart."

Bitterness in my heart? It seems like a strange thing to say.

"Fates, Mom," I mutter. "Isn't it a bit early in the morning for you to be lecturing me about the state of my heart?"

"Yes, he needs another croissant for that," Mrs. A says indulgently.

I take her words as permission to pilfer another one. She pours me a giant glass of milk to wash it down.

"What you really need is more protein. Is this all you've eaten today?" Mrs. A asks.

"I'm okay," I mutter, downing the glass of milk. "Not hungry today."

"You couldn't sleep, and you're not hungry." My mom stops what she's doing and puts her hands on her hips. "What do I need to know about this fight last week?"

"Nothing." Fuck. I grab another croissant and stuff it in my mouth to avoid further discussion. I'm saved by the sound of a delivery truck pulling up in the back alley.

"There's your Monday delivery." I push open the back door and walk out to help.

It's not like my mom and Mrs. A are wimps. They're shifters, so they're a lot stronger than human females their respective ages, but helping with heavy things is the chivalrous thing to do for the she-wolves in your life.

And these two she-wolves are the only people I've ever had in my corner.

* * *

Lotta

I splash cold water on my face before my last class. I'm barely functional today. I didn't sleep last night. I'm starving but couldn't eat breakfast or lunch because I'm nauseous as hell.

My fingers are trembly. I'm feverish.

I have that itchy feeling like I'm going to spontaneously shift again like I did the night of the full moon.

And now I'm terrified that the scent or sight of Asher in the next class will bring on something even worse. Some kind of shameful public spectacle that will lose me this job and forever shame me and my family.

I pick at the fabric of my T shirt at my sternum, pulling it out and in to fan myself and cool the sweat between my breasts.

The deep breath I draw to clear my head only makes me dizzy. And the worst part of all is the frantic thrum between my legs. The wetness there as I review over and over how it felt to be taken by the man who is my mate. The man who is barely a man.

The one who left me needy and wound up last night. And that neediness has now festered into a full fledged sickness.

I grab a paper towel and pat my face, staring at my bright eyes and flushed cheeks in the mirror.

That queasiness in the pit of my stomach churns as I think about seeing Asher. He did this on purpose. I thought it was a torture to male wolves to meet a mate and not claim her, but somehow, he's turned the tables on me.

He's gloating right now over what he did last night. Nipping and sucking up my inner thigh, putting his hot mouth directly over my core.

I clutch the sink as an orgasm runs through me. It's completely unsatisfying though. The kind that only builds my need and heat.

Just get through sixth period. Then you can shift and run.

I push off from the sink and walk on shaky legs to the door. My spine stiffens as I march out of the faculty bathroom and into my classroom.

The bell rings, but Asher and his entourage don't stop their goofing around in the back of my classroom.

"*In your seats,*" I snarl with more force than the situation calls for. The class goes silent, everyone staring at me curiously as those who hadn't sat down now slide into their seats.

"Who pissed in your Cheerios?" Asher mutters to his friends. They snicker in reply.

I bite my cheek so hard it bleeds. I make them all suffer in dead silence as I take attendance. Even after I'm done, I fix them with a stony stare for several long moments before I clip, "Work on your self-portraits."

I disappear to the corner of the studio where I've set up two giant canvases as a partition for my privacy when I paint. I don't usually go here during class—it's unprofessional to leave the class unsupervised, but I need a moment. I kick off my heeled sandals. I'm too wobbly to navigate walking with them.

Get it together, Lotta. Don't show weakness. Don't let Asher think he's won.

After drawing several deep breaths, I grab the mason jar, muddy with yesterday's paint and brushes, and carry it back out in the classroom to the sink.

The volume in the class has steadily grown. Somehow everyone realized I won't be teaching today, and they've clearly decided not to work. Or rather, they're pretending to work as they talk.

A wave of heat rolls over me as I swish the brushes in the thinner. I immediately understand why. The hulking form of my worst student has appeared beside me. Asher pretends to look through the stack of magazines I have out for multimedia work.

"Your smell is off." His voice is low—barely audible to me, which means no one else in the room should be able to hear him, shifter hearing or not.

"*You* did this to me," I whisper-snarl. I don't look his way. If anyone glanced over they would see our backs angled away from each other. Two people near each other but not interacting.

He edges a little closer, reaching above me to open the cabinets above my head. His cedar and soap scent assaults me. The tension rippling through my body is too much. My fingers close in a fist around the mason jar, and I accidentally crush it in a superhuman grip.

I gasp as the glass shatters, jamming into the fleshy part of my thumb. Half of the pieces fall into the sink, the other half fall over my bare feet.

"What the fuck?"

Before I can even move, Asher picks me up by the waist and plops my ass down on the counter beside the sink.

"Why are you in your bare feet?" He sounds angry, like I'm giving him personal offense by showing my toes. But who knows what's going through his mind right now. He probably hates the protectiveness his wolf would display over me getting hurt.

"Somebody clean that glass from the floor," Asher orders and four students scramble to comply.

I move to hop down, my face flaming. "You don't pick up a teacher, no matter how chivalrous you think you're bei —Oh." I suck in a sharp gasp. "What do you think you're doing?"

Asher rips his T-shirt off, and he holds it beneath my hand, using it as a rag to soak up my blood. There's nothing wrong with that instinct, *per se,* except that it leaves his torso bared to me.

And his chest is magnificent. The strong, sculpted pectorals are lightly dusted with golden curls. His flat nipples are taut. His scent is everywhere now, coating my face. I can't breathe any air that doesn't smell like him.

He bends over my hand to take a closer look, and pulls a shard of glass from my bleeding flesh.

The room tilts and spins. The air feels thick.

He's touching me. This is what I needed. What I've been needing since the moment he walked out my door last night.

He pulls another piece of glass out of my hand, then stretches my wrist toward the sink.

I can't think. Can't function with him this close. It feels like my body is going to erupt right here in the classroom.

"Enough," I snap, hopping off the counter and onto the floor, glass underfoot be damned. "Class, I'm going to take care of this cut. Keep working *quietly.*"

I beeline it out of the room in my bare feet, blood dripping in my wake. I don't look back to see if the class is going to follow my instructions. I definitely don't look back to see Asher's reaction.

I don't think I can withstand the view of his beautiful angry visage.

I unlock and shove open the door to the faculty bathroom. My heart pounds at an uneven rhythm. My head swims. I can't think.

I pace in a tight swift circle. The air feels too thick to breathe. I stop in front of the sink and turn the water on. Blood washes into the basin as I rinse the rest of the glass from my thumb. My chest heaves as I try to regain control.

But that's an impossibility.

I must not have shut the automatically locking door when I came in because Asher somehow appears in the bathroom with me.

I stare as he shuts the door with a click and closes the distance between us in one long stride.

He tears off my shirt and throws it to the floor.

Chapter Ten

Lotta

I mean to tell him to get out. He shouldn't have followed me in here. *We're at school!* I can't be seen with a student.

But none of those words come from my lips. My hands fly to his shorts, fingers fumbling with the button.

His mouth is on my breast, lips locking around my nipple. I don't even know how he got there so fast.

He pins my body against the wall, one hand cupping my ass to boost me up. I prop a foot up against the double sink, parting my legs for him.

I work his erection free from his shorts and boxer briefs and use it like a handle to drag his hips toward mine.

"You need me to fuck you?" Asher's muttered words are gravely, skidding out his lips between pants. He seems as frantic as I am, as desperate to get relief.

He yanks my skirt up to my waist and shoves his hand down my panties, rubbing a finger between my legs. I kick out of the panties and push his hand away. It's not his fingers I need right now. I certainly don't require foreplay.

I'm about sixteen hours past the foreplay stage. Well beyond the female equivalent of blue balls, whatever that may be called. It feels like someone punched me in the vagina. My clit is so engorged it hurts.

"You need this cock?" He barely breathes the words in my ear.

"Yes," I snarl, teeth bared. I close my eyes and lean my head back against the wall, so I don't have to look at the proud planes of Asher's handsome face so close to mine.

I don't want this. I need it, but I don't want it.

He spears me with his length, driving my hips up the wall to take him deeply. His exhale hits my ear with a hot blast.

I choke back a cry of satisfaction. "Oh fate," I whisper.

He shoves in again.

My eyes roll back in my head. "Oh fate, oh fate, oh fate."

This is everything I needed. No, it's more than that—it's glorious.

I wrap my free leg around his waist, so he can bounce me over his erection, my pelvis angled toward him.

"Yeah," I mutter.

Asher's thumb finds my lower lip, and he traces it then penetrates me there, too. I suck hard on his digit, scrape my teeth over the skin.

My core contracts around his cock on each instroke.

The sensation of Asher pumping into me is better than finding out I got into art school. Better than leaving Wolf Ridge. Better than winning first prize in our college art show.

It has the sensation and significance of life purpose. Like all I ever will need is *this*. As if I could die in this moment and be complete.

But that's just biology, I remind myself. It's not real. This isn't the real me.

This feeling will fade when we're done, and I can figure out how to never do this again.

Lies, my wolf snarls.

Tears spear my eyes. I dig my nails into Asher's built shoulders and use my foot on the sink to leverage my hips to meet his.

Asher stifles his groan. Both of us are in a muffled frenzy of panting breath and silent sobs. If someone walked by, they would only hear the water still running in the sink.

Tears streak my face. I'm not sure what they're from—sexual frustration, maybe. Disappointment and anger with myself for losing control this way. For being so needy. For letting a student of mine—a *student*!—hate fuck me against a wall in a bathroom during the middle of class.

I bite down hard on Asher's thumb, breaking the skin. He yanks it out of my mouth. I open my eyes to watch his eyes change from bright wolf green—back to hazel.

"Come." I shake his shoulders. The tears are falling fast now. "I need to come."

I watch a flare of panic cross Asher's face. That's when I realize we're not using protection.

Fate, what is wrong with me? I've truly lost my mind!

He slowly marshals the wantonness in his expression, the strong jaw turning steely, his eyes narrowing. He shoves into me and stops moving. I start to protest, but he slides the pad of his thumb to my clit, and I go over the edge with a shriek. I muffle it by biting into Asher's shoulder as I come and come and come.

He remains stiff—heh—and unmoving, letting me grind and grind against his root until the last of my orgasm has been wrenched free.

The moment I'm done, he lifts me off his cock and drops me to my feet, then he fists his cock and aims it toward the sink.

The ropey muscles of his back bunch and tense, and then he comes, the ribbons of his essence washing down the drain under the steam of running water.

My brain clears. Asher's so smart. I pant in barely more than a whisper, "Wash my scent off your dick."

I turn on the sink closest to me and run water over my hands. I still can't stop the silent tears over the helplessness I feel. The sense that my body betrayed me.

Asher turns, and his brows slam down. He reaches for me. I don't know what he intends—to wipe my tears or cradle my cheek or some other such bullshit, but I'm not having it.

I slap his hand away and turn to pick up my panties from the floor.

I don't make it there. Asher picks me up with an arm around my waist, and he throws me against the stall wall.

Two of his meaty fingers sink between my legs.

I gasp at the delicious sensation, my quenched need flaming bright again.

Asher closes the fingers of his other hand around my throat. His mouth crashes down on mine. I turn my head, but he chases my mouth, prying my lips open with his tongue. He lashes me with it, plunging deep into my mouth, simultaneously penetrating me in both places.

He's angry, but I'm not sure why.

It doesn't matter. I'm already in the throes of ecstasy. His cedar and soap scent drugs me as his fingers work their magic. He isn't choking me, just holding me in place. Dominating me. Reminding me how powerless I am against him. If he wanted to fuck me in this bathroom for the next forty-eight hours straight, I'd submit, unable to refuse the potent pleasure he's capable of wringing from me.

I clap a hand over my own mouth to muffle the cry of victory that issues from my lips as I reach my second peak. My internal muscles clamp around his fingers. I bring my own fingers there to press him in deeper and rub my clit.

"Go back to class, Asher," I say through a clogged throat. My tears have stopped though. I guess eventually the pleasure outweighs the agony.

I'm still grinding on his knuckles as I give the command.

Asher takes his time easing out of me, his lips twisted into a cruel smirk. It's made even crueler by the two dimples that make him Hollywood-worthy. It's like my brain can't compute that anyone that good-looking could also be such an ass. "All right, Ms. James. But I expect an A on that missing assignment." He's all swagger as he walks to the sink to wash my scent from his fingers. He looks over his shoulder at me. "And all other assignments henceforth."

* * *

Asher

"Too much force!" Coach Jamison bellows as I run down the field, knocking player after player so hard I send them flying overhead.

He races down the field and grabs me by the helmet to get my attention. I slow my run to a stop, and he swings me to face him and gives the helmet a shake. "Put your wolf away, Asher. What has gotten into you? You can't do that on my field. You're *at school* right now."

"I'm sorry, Coach."

"What is going on with you?"

I shake my head.

"Don't bullshit me. You got suspended for fighting last week. Now you're back but seem to be looking for another round with someone. Am I right?"

I shake my head. "No, Coach. It's not like that."

"Well, how is it then?" He stares at me.

My chest feels heavy with his disappointment. Coach Jamison is the closest thing I have to a dad now, so when he's up in my grill, I pay attention.

"I'm sorry. I didn't realize how hard I was hitting." It's not true but also not a complete lie. I wasn't paying attention because I didn't care. It doesn't matter. No one out on our field is human. If I hurt any of them they will heal by morning.

Hurt. Fuck.

The memory of Lotta's blood spilling into the sink flashes in front of my eyes, and my wolf snarls beneath the surface. I want to flatten some more of my teammates.

Of course, she's fine. The cut was already closed by the time I joined her in the bathroom.

But I'm still fucking traumatized by her tears.

I know she wanted what I gave her. I'm damn sure it was consensual. She just didn't *want* to want it. But to watch the girl of your dreams cry while you fuck her hard against a wall is more than unnerving. It disturbed me to my core.

"*That.*" Coach Jamison claps a hand against my helmet. "What are you thinking about, Asher?"

"Nothing, Coach."

"So we lie to each other now? Is that how it is?" He pins me with a penetrating stare. It's not his pack dominance that gets to me. It's the fact that he cares.

He's one of the very few people in this town who gives a

shit about what happens to me. Who doesn't lump me in with my no-good dad.

Fuck.

"It's a girl," I admit. I'm obviously not going to say which girl.

He waits without any reaction. Apparently that wasn't enough of an explanation.

"We hooked up on the full moon run."

"Without protection." The disappointment in his tone is clear. I swear Coach Jamison takes his unofficial job as the team's sex educator more seriously than training us for football.

"I pulled out."

Coach shakes his head. "Not effective. How many times have I told you guys that?"

"Every full moon for the last four years," I mutter. I should be shamed by Coach's admonishment, but instead, a warm contented feeling is soaking through my PTSD from this afternoon.

But why?

I look around to see if Lotta is nearby.

I don't see her. It's just the team out here. Then I realize–

It's Coach's fear that I impregnated her. My wolf is responding to that idea with deep satisfaction. Like knocking up the art teacher at my high school is a good idea. Like she would ever want to have a family with me.

Keep her.

I hear the delusional whisper in my head.

But I don't get to keep this girl. I don't even want to keep her. I despise Lotta James for what she did.

I may desire her sexually, but that's it. I will never get

past what she did. I won't forgive her for it–not that she's even asked for my forgiveness.

Besides, she can't be with a student. She'd be fired if anyone found out.

"Morning after pill might still be an option. Dr. Oakley understands about the pull of a full moon. Doesn't he stock that cabin of his with condoms for you kids?"

It's true–Abe's dad has made it clear since we were in middle school that his cabin is available for any of us. He's another Wolf Ridge evangelist for safe sex.

"Yeah. I didn't make it to the cabin."

Coach Jamison peers at me. "You like this girl?"

I shake my head. "No."

He lifts his brows. "Want to talk about it?"

I look away, scanning my buddies on the field. "No."

"Asher, you're more than this. You don't have to fit in the hole this town wants to put you in. I've been telling you, a football scholarship to ASU is still possible. Maybe even UCLA. Their scout was watching you. But not if you're getting yourself suspended. And not if you knock a she-wolf up."

"I know, Coach. I'm sorry."

"That's nice, but I don't need your apology, Asher. You need to figure out who you really owe an apology to."

I shake my head as he stalks away, not wanting to analyze the puzzle he dropped. But like all the mind-wedgies he inflicts on the team, I'm sure I'll be working it out over the next few weeks.

Well, I'm sure as hell not going to apologize to Lotta if that's what he meant.

The best that female will ever get from me will be a rough fuck and a slap on the ass.

Chapter Eleven

Lotta

I sit on Dr. Oakley's examination table and scroll through Instagram. I haven't posted a new painting in a month, but my channel is full of wolf paintings. If the pack knew I was putting these up for the world to see, Alpha Green and the other elders would freak. Our species is careful about hiding our secret. Understandably.

The U.S. Government knows we exist—just like they know alien life exists and has visited Earth. Some say they keep a record of packs and their members in America. I don't know whether that's true. I do know there have been shifters who have been snatched and subjected to grievous testing, and government-funded experimentation. I've also heard there are special ops teams in the U.S. military that consist entirely of shifters. Kind of like Navy SEALs 2.0.

Regardless, one of the primary pack rules is to hide our existence from other humans. So me posting canvas after canvas of the larger-than-life-sized wolves I paint would be frowned on. Especially the ones that show an overlay of a human on the wolf. The meaning might be too obvious, even to a human.

My favorite art professor, Ann Sweetling, thought I was depicting a person's inner wolf spirit or animal spirit guide. That's the angle I play up on my Instagram page, and I've sold a number of the paintings. I guess a lot of those woo-woo people out there think they have a wolf animal spirit.

If only they knew what it's like to actually be run by your wolf.

Just thinking of my other side makes me break out in a sweat.

A light tap sounds on the door, and Dr. Oakley and his female assistant, Melinda, enter.

"Carlotta," Dr. Oakley says warmly. "I'd heard you were back. It's good to see you." He takes a quick sweep of my body before meeting my eyes. "You're looking...are you feeling all right?"

I glance at Melinda. Her daughter is a friend of mine–we graduated from Wolf Ridge the same year. The trouble with small towns is that your business becomes everyone's business in about four hours.

"Melinda is here so you feel comfortable with any examination I conduct, and by law, everything we discuss in this room is confidential. You're an adult, which means we can't discuss anything with your parents or anyone else without your consent."

I nod and draw a breath. "To be honest, the full moon kicked my butt. I hadn't shifted since I left for college, and this feels like a second puberty or transition."

"Check her blood pressure," he directs Melinda, who jumps into action.

"You suppressed your wolf the entire time you were away?" To his credit, he covers his surprise fairly quickly.

"Yes."

"Did that cause any adverse symptoms?"

"Loss of appetite and energy. Some hair loss. Low-level depression. But after about nine months, I got used to it."

"Nine months is a long time to be feeling unwell. That must've been hard on you."

It's been so long, but his sympathy brings back that intense loneliness I suffered. The grief over my parents' abandonment was made even harder by the grief from my wolf.

Melinda reads off my blood pressure, but the numbers mean nothing to me. Shifters don't need doctors except for birth control or massive trauma. The last time I saw Dr. Oakley was as a freshman in high school to get on birth control for the full moon runs.

Same reason I'm back now.

"I had to do it. I wanted to pursue an education in art, and the best school was in Chicago. It was the only way I could cope with living amongst humans."

Dr. Oakley raises a brow as if to say he disagrees with my reasoning, but he doesn't argue. I supposed he lived amongst humans for years getting his medical degree, too.

He brings the stethoscope to my chest and listens. "So you shifted for the first time again—when? With the full moon?"

"Yes, sir."

He waves a hand. "You don't need to call me *sir*. When you're in this office there's no pack hierarchy or tradition."

I lower my gaze, just the same. I may be an adult, but respect for elders has been thoroughly bred into me. "Thank you."

"And now you're experiencing hot flashes? Extreme hunger? Low blood sugar?"

"Yes." I swallow and nod. I leave out the part about Asher. About my desperation to feel him inside me, riding me hard. My intense need to crawl all over that muscled body of his. To have him master me with dirty-talk and rough handling.

"Well, I expect it will be just like the onset of your wolf again. I don't think it will last as long as puberty. I would think since you've been through it before, and you know how to shift between forms and how much food and exercise your wolf requires, you should adjust in a matter of a few months."

"Months?"

He shrugs. "Two to three would be my guess, but it's only a guess. You're thin, Carlotta. I would say get as much protein and fat into your body as you can to help stabilize the return of the hormones."

"Okay."

"Anything else?"

"I need to get back on birth control."

"Okay." He glances at my chart. "It looks like we stopped mailing your formulation to you six months ago."

Dr. Oakley works with a compounding pharmacist to make special formulations that will work with shifter hormones.

The only reason I stopped taking it was to keep myself from having gratuitous sex with my self-absorbed roommate, Andy. He was good-looking and available but completely conceited and empty in the brain department. I knew the roommates with benefits thing was a bad idea, but I indulged.

Obviously, I was using him. When I started feeling used back, I realized the relationship wasn't healthy for either of us, and I cut off the sex. To keep myself from the temptation of returning, I went off the pill.

"Do you need a post-full moon shot?"

This is Dr. Oakley's bread and butter, if I had to guess. Except I don't know if he even charges anyone for it. His primary contribution to the pack is keeping teen wolves from getting pregnant during full moon runs.

It's hard enough to keep your wolf under control, but when you're a new shifter and the moon is full, nature takes over.

The post full moon shot is like the morning-after pill for humans.

"Yes, please."

Dr. Oakley nods at Melinda, who is already pulling out a syringe and alcohol swab. She rips open the swab packet and paints it on my shoulder.

"This may help stabilize your hormones," Dr. Oakley says. "Or it could make it temporarily worse." He takes the needle from Melinda and jabs me. "Hard to say." He pulls the needle out and disposes of it.

I'm sweating and hot. Itchy like I need to shift and run.

"I suggest you get plenty of rest and increase your caloric intake."

"Got it." I hop off the table, eager to get out of there.

"And Carlotta" –he turns at the door to give me a smile– "Welcome home."

My stomach tightens up into a fist as I force a smile. "Thanks, but I don't intend to stay."

His brows shoot up. "No?"

"Wolf Ridge isn't my home anymore."

* * *

Asher

There are at least ten things I should be doing tonight that don't involve stalking Lotta. I have a fuck-ton of homework to make up from the days I was suspended. My mom asked me to replace the broken screen protector on her phone. Seb offered to help me with the math test I need to retake.

Instead, I'm creeping up on Lotta's back porch, dying for the hit of her jasmine and honey scent.

I already fucked her today. I shouldn't need more.

She shouldn't need more.

But what if she does? My wolf murmurs in my head.

She was tortured when I came into her class today. I did that to her. By denying us both last night, I caused her obvious harm. Pain, even.

That knowledge is a torture in itself. It makes me itchy. Uneasy. I wouldn't call it guilt. More like the physiological version of guilt. My body regrets and mourns any pain I caused her beautiful body.

And that must be the reason I'm looking in her dark windows and trying her locked door right now.

The lights are off in her place. It's not that late, but maybe she was exhausted from whatever physical ordeal she went through today. More unease creeps through me.

I tap lightly on the door. I don't hear anything from inside. That's when I spot one of her flip flops in the brush.

My wolf roars to the surface. I nearly shift with the idea that she's in danger. But that's dumb. There's no reason to assume that. Fuck. I can't stop the roar of energy holding through my body. The need to find her.

I snatch up the shoe and scan the surroundings. The other shoe is farther down the wash. And then–oh fuck!

Her shorts are caught on a small palo verde. There's her shirt.

I strip out of my clothes on the spot and shift, following her scent trail up the mountain. I race up the hillside. My mate shifted in a hurry. Like something was chasing her. Like something was wrong. I don't smell any other fresh scent near hers, though.

Something's wrong with her wolf, then.

That's why she was so off today.

Maybe it had nothing to do with me. No—it *was* about me. I'm the one who fixed it for her. Her body craved mine the same way mine craves hers. She needed me to fuck her hard to straighten her out.

I continue my hunt, climbing steadily in elevation. She must've had a good head start on me because it takes me a long time to catch up, and I'm running fast. My wolf is far more powerful and strong than hers.

Finally I see her under the waning moon. The slender white wolf leans against a boulder, sides heaving like she's exhausted.

Mine, my wolf snarls.

I let myself have her. Again.

I shift and stride toward her. My dick is harder than steel, pointing in the direction of its desire.

"Shift," I command.

She's powerless against me. She instantly transforms, rising to two shaky legs, green eyes changing back to cornflower blue. Her long dark waves fall across one shoulder, sliding against her pert breast.

I pick her up by the waist. A cry comes from her lips, but it's not a protest. It sounds needier than that. I climb a few steps up to the top of the boulder, where I gently lie her back on the flat surface. Her skin glows under the moonlight, giving her an ethereal quality. Like she's the moon goddess herself, come down to Earth to experience carnal pleasure.

I kneel and slide my hands behind her knees to push them up, spreading her wide. Her belly shudders in and out as I lower my head.

I hold her gaze for a moment, a silent question of consent.

"*Yes.*" Her answer is impatient. She understands the question.

My thumbs tighten around her legs reflexively. My dick throbs. I won't be able to stop myself from fucking her. I can try to delay it, though. Try to keep my head.

I part her folds with my tongue, delving between those sweet peach halves. She tastes like sunshine. Like honey. Maybe I will be able to hold back after all. Right now, I'm pretty sure I could spend the next five hours tasting her.

She moans. Her knees press inward, powerful, her powerful inner thighs fighting my grip. Her hips roll up to meet me. The sound she makes as I trace inside her lips is a guttural *Ahhh*.

I love you.

That's the thought that pops in my head, which is an utter lie.

I don't love her. I hate her.

Yet, my wolf is singing this serenade to her in my head. *Beautiful, beautiful female. I adore you. I have always adored you. You are the light of the moon. You are the song on the wind. You are the catch in my throat.*

I work her clit with the level of reverence my wolf feels for this female. I praise her with the tip of my tongue. I lave her. I stroke and soothe and aim to stupify her with the prowess of my mouth's devotion.

Her legs tremble and shake around my shoulders. Her fingers thread into my hair and pull. The *ahhh* sounds spill from her lips in a continuous articulation of joy.

"That's it, sweetheart." I lift my head and shift my hands to slide two fingers inside her. I don't mean to sweet talk her–the words tumbled out of my mouth. I guess they are a truthful expression of the moment.

I thrust in and slide my fingers along her inner wall, seeking that secret location. The bundle of nerves that collect around the G-spot.

Lotta arches when I find it, a cry issuing from her throat. Fluid gushes around my fingers in the most glorious female ejaculation I've ever had the honor of witnessing. Her muscles pulse around my fingers with her orgasm, a spasmodic dance of victory.

I keep my fingers inside her and lower my face once more, adding my tongue to the mix. She contracts around my fingers, lifting her hips from the boulder, her legs looping over my shoulders.

"Tastes like heaven," I murmur. I let my fingers slip out, and she sighs as they leave.

"More," she pants.

Of course, she wants more. I mean, thank fuck because I definitely want more. But it's like we can't get enough of each other.

Maybe that's the denial of a claiming bite–I don't know. All I'm sure of is that I will combust soon if I don't get inside her again.

It's rough out here, though. I don't want to pound into her against rocks.

"Come here." I grasp her hand and pull her to her feet. Once she's up, I catch her waist and carry her off the boulder, back to solid ground. "Hands on the rock." I fold her in half, pulling back on her hips, so her hands fall to the boulder. "Stick that pretty ass out for me."

I give her ass a firm smack.

She moans.

I spank her some more. I remember how much she likes it. It's a shame there's not enough moonlight to watch my handprints bloom on that soft skin of hers.

Punishing her gets me way too excited. Pre-cum drips from the tip of my cock. If I don't get inside her soon, I fear I will lose control and mark her right here.

And I definitely have no plans to mark this female.

I grab her ass cheeks and spread her wide to bring my cock to her entrance. It doesn't even require my guidance to get in. One snap of my hips, and I've penetrated those plump folds. I press in deeper, going slowly until I reach the hilt. She moans her content, but I stay there, torturing both of us with my restraint.

She pushes back against me to take me deeper. She's so wet. My cock slides through her juices to delicious perfection.

I start a slow rhythm–short bumps against her ass. I still have her cheeks spread wide, so she gets the contact of my loins against her anus.

Her cry is surprised and frantic, as if she's already nearing a second climax just from me being inside her.

I can relate. I don't know how long I'll last before I have to pull out and come all over her ass.

I take longer, slower, strokes, building the tension for both of us.

"Asher," Lotta gasps. "I need..."

I pull out and wrap an arm under her torso, squeezing one breast roughly as I deliver a flurry of hard spanks to her upturned ass. "I know what you need," I growl. I spank her even harder, catching the backs of her legs where ass meets thigh. "I fucking know what you need. I'm your goddamn mate."

"I know, I know," she pants. "Please." I love that she's begging now. "Give it to me. Please Asher. I need it."

My cock is so hard it feels like it will burst. My sanity is slipping.

"Okay, baby. Hands on the ground. Fold all the way over, now." I pull her hips back and make her take a step away from the boulder, so there's room for her hands to drop to the foot of the rock.

Her legs are shaking hard, but I kick them wider and hold her steady to position her in a downward dog pike position. When I enter her from this angle, I get in deep.

She shrieks her pleasure. "Yes!"

"I know." I grip her hips and bang her hard.

She bends her knees to brace against my thrusts, arching back, driving into me as I drive into her.

"Uhn. You feel so good," I groan. I slap my hips against hers, loving the sound of flesh colliding with flesh. Loving the sight of this slip of a female arched to receive me. "I just *can't* with this ass." I slide my thumbs around to tug her asscheeks open again.

She cries out at the sensation. "Asher! Oh, Fate. Please! Please!"

I want to come inside her so badly, but, of course, it's out of the question. I squeeze my eyes closed and meter breath through my nostrils to hold off. A little longer. I don't want it to end.

Somehow my brain cobbles together a plan for us to orgasm together. I pull out of her and shove three fingers into her sopping channel, pressing her anus with my thumb. She climaxes hard around my fingers at the same time I fist my cock with the other hand and coat her beautiful ass with cum.

We both vocalize our release, our voices an offering up to the wind. To the silver moon. To the mountain.

I coax out another release and then another from each of us, waiting until the last one dies, and then shifting the position of my fingers to trigger the next.

When at last it seems we've both wrung out every last drop of ecstasy, I slide my fingers out of my beautiful mate and help her to stand. Her legs don't hold her, though. She looks up at me, her eyelids flutter, and then she collapses against my body in a dead slump.

Chapter Twelve

Lotta

The scent of my mate.

Trees brushing against my skin.

Jostled movement.

The sound of running water.

I only catch snippets of consciousness until I find myself enveloped in warm water.

I crack my eyes open and blink, looking around. I'm in my bathtub. Asher crouches beside me, soothing the flush from my face with a cool washcloth. He fills out his worn, faded Wolf Ridge t-shirt in an indecent, delectable way.

Oh, Fate–the way he took me tonight. I turn my palms up to see if the skin is still torn from pushing against the rock.

It is. I haven't healed yet. Something's wrong with me.

My stomach rumbles.

"What happened?" I try to sit up. Try to take charge of the situation. I absolutely hate how out of control I feel around Asher. Because of Asher.

He puts two fingers against my sternum. With just

those two fingers, he applies enough pressure to keep me firmly in place. "Don't move yet. You passed out. When was the last time you ate?"

"I had dinner," I say, but when I remember the meager serving of carrots and hummus I ate, I realize Asher's probably right. All the shifting and the sex requires way more calories than I'm used to consuming. My blood sugar must've tanked.

"Why am I in the bath?"

"I wasn't sure if you wanted to go to bed with my cum smeared all over your ass." His voice is dry, but there's a line between his brows, and the tenderness with which he applies the washcloth belies the gruffness.

Asher stands. "I'm going to go find you some food. *Do not* leave that bath." He arches his brows in a sexy-stern way that makes me melt deeper into the water.

When did the boy-next-door become this huge, bossy man? It occurs to me that I don't know Asher at all. I remember a defensive kid suffering in school because of an unstable home environment related to his dad. I took on the volunteer tutoring job to improve my chances of winning a scholarship to art school, and it was tough at first. He barely spoke to me the first semester I worked with him.

But I persevered. I worked with him three days a week. By Christmas, he'd leveled up in math, and the rest of his grades were above a C. But the real change was the trust that developed between us.

A trust I completely violated.

I lean my head back against the tile and close my eyes. Regret and pain wash over me. For someone who used to be a pack princess, my life is now a tangled mess.

The scent of butter and toast wafts in, and I sense my body's relief. I'm going to be fed.

I have to admit, after over four years completely on my own, cut off from the support of my parents, it feels almost too good to be taken care of by someone. It's especially dangerous when that someone is the guy who just hate-fucked me on the mountain. And in the school bathroom.

Ugh! I still can't believe I did that. It's so shameful. So wrong.

After a few minutes, Asher enters with a plate piled high with grilled cheese sandwiches. "There's no food in your place," he grumbles. He sets the plate down on the side of the bathtub.

I reach for one of the buttery toasted cheese sandwiches that smell like pure heaven, my stomach gurgling loudly.

Asher leans a hip against the sink, his arms folded across his massive chest. "You know you're a wolf, right?"

I ignore him, barely chewing the food as I inhale it.

"Why is there no meat in your refrigerator? Are you trying to be a vegetarian or something?"

I don't answer. I want to tell him to leave, but I don't have the energy to assert myself yet. I finish the first sandwich, and my hands stop shaking. By the second one, I feel more like myself.

I try to get up, but Asher shakes his head. For some insane reason, my body obeys his dominance, and I freeze.

"Finish the other two, then we'll talk about you moving."

I oblige him, reaching for a third beautiful grilled cheese.

"Lotta." There's a weighted tone to his voice that brings my gaze to his for the first time since I regained consciousness. But he doesn't say anything about us. About this thing we're doing that absolutely needs to stop. About how we should handle it or what we should do. He's still stuck on the food. "Why aren't you eating?"

I give an impatient wave of my hand that knocks the plate off the side of the tub.

Asher's reflexes are lightning fast. He catches the plate and rights it before the remaining sandwich flies off the edge.

"Whoa. Impressive."

"What's the deal, Lotta? Talk, or you're not getting out of that tub."

I roll my eyes. "You can't hold me prisoner in my bathtub, Asher. You know one yell and my parents would be here and–" I stop my threat because we both know where things would go if I did that. Asher would be booted out of the pack just like his father. My mom would make it happen before morning. And of course, that line of thinking brings back our twisted history and the reason he hates me now.

He takes a bite of the last sandwich. "And?" he asks with his mouth full, his cocky demeanor in full force. "You gonna finish that sentence?"

My face flushes and then grows suddenly tight, like I'm going to cry again. But this time it isn't about feeling helpless to my wolf urges. It's from the power and potency of Asher's wrath. I feel it hit me square in the chest and take my breath away. A blast of hatred that makes me want to curl up in a ball.

"No." I throw a note of stubbornness in my voice, blinking back the tears.

"Tell me about the food. I don't get it."

I finish my third sandwich, and Asher thrusts his half-eaten one in my face, offering me what's left.

I shake my head, but my fingers reach for the food

anyway, my hunger still unquenched. "I haven't shifted in almost five years," I admit as I chew the food.

Asher cocks his head. *"What?"*

I shrug. "I lived in the heart of Chicago. There was no way I could hide as a wolf there."

"So you just...didn't? You suppressed your wolf?"

I swallow and nod. "Yep. That's how I managed living among humans."

Asher's eyes narrow. "Is that why you didn't come back for summers or breaks?"

"Yes. It would've been too hard to let her out and then suppress her again. I went through withdrawal symptoms when I first got there. I was sick for nine months. I lost my appetite and got really thin."

I finish the last bite of the sandwich. Asher sets the plate down on the sink and reaches for me. Before I know it's happening, he's lifted me by my armpits out of the bath and set me onto the bathmat.

"You're still really thin, Lotta." He wraps a towel around my back but holds it open to examine my naked body.

It should anger me, this forced vulnerability. I should feel the defensiveness my mom's constant criticism or input about me, my life, and my body does, but instead, his perusal warms me. I sense only a mate's caring and concern from him. No judgment.

He uses the towel to tug me closer to him, my wet skin almost flush to his body. Close enough that some of my water droplets transfer to his clothes. I start to tremble again but not from weakness. "You shifted for *me*." His gravelly voice sounds possessive. His eyes glow green. The electricity between our bodies is undeniable. Like the strings of an instrument, tuned to the same note. Reverberating at the same frequency and speed.

I put my hands on his chest and push myself back, desperately needing space. "Probably," I mutter, turning away. "I didn't mean to let her out again. I don't plan to stay in Wolf Ridge."

I hear the catch of his breath when I deliver that news, but I don't see his reaction because I walk out of the bathroom to my dresser in the studio, where I pull out a fresh pair of panties.

Asher follows, watching me with those glowing wolf-eyes as I slip on the panties, a cami, and pajama shorts.

"Well, you need meat. I'm sure you know that."

"I know, but meat's expensive. I can't afford it."

Asher's eyes narrow, and he looks toward the French doors that open to the pool and my parent's million dollar property. "Why not?"

I've recovered now. My strength is back and so is my determination.

I march over to Asher and stop in front of him with my hands on my hips. He's a foot taller than I am, so I have to look up to glare at him.

"All right, here's the deal. You brought my wolf out. I clearly need" –I stop and wave my hand in the air, trying to conjure the right words– "sex now."

Asher's eyes light with new interest. "*Now*? Did you stop having sex for five years, too?"

"No!" I try and fail to give him a shove. I only succeed in knocking myself backward. "Listen, Asher. We need some ground rules."

I'm surprised when he nods. "Okay. Like what?"

"One:" –I hold up my finger– "Never at school again. That *cannot* happen." I hold up another finger. "Two: No one else knows." Alarm suddenly rings through me. "Have you told anyone?"

"That I fucked you?" He scowls, that sculpted chest stiffening. "Of course not."

"Good. Keep it that way. And three:" –I add a digit– "Only here, only after dark, and no one sees you coming or going."

Asher catches the wrist of the hand I'm holding up and brings my knuckles to his mouth. He bites them–harder than a nip, but not actually painful. "I agree to your demands. Here are mine." He sucks one of my fingers into his mouth, and my body's instantly on fire again. I still feel the twinges between my legs from our previous two rounds today. My body can't possibly crave more.

But it does.

He releases my finger from his mouth with a pop of his lips. "Your body belongs to me. Anyone else touches it, they die."

The intimate muscles between my legs lift and contract. My heart inexplicably starts to pound.

He sucks another finger and releases it. "I get to do whatever the fuck I want with you. If I want to kiss you–" He loops a hand behind my head and lifts my face to his. His lips descend and hover, millimeters away from mine, his hot breath feathering across my face. "—you open these lips for me." He attacks my mouth, his tongue sweeping between my lips, possessing me.

I struggle–or rather, part of me struggles while part of me submits. And the third part of me just ignites into white hot flames.

He breaks the kiss by dragging my lower lip between his teeth.

"If I want to fuck you, you open those legs."

Said legs wobble, barely holding me up. The worst part is that I'm sure he knows his effect on me. He can smell my arousal. Feel the way I melt into him despite my deep desire to resist.

"And if you ever slap my hand away again when I want to caress you, I will spank you until you cry. Understand?"

My nipples pucker. A powerful shiver rolls through my body. I'm equal parts furious and turned on. I want to knee him in the balls. I also sort of *want* that spanking.

Why does that turn me on so much? Do I *desire* his punishment for what I did?

Face hot, palms wet, the best response I can manage is to spit out three words: "I hate you."

A slow, smug grin spreads across Asher's face. "Believe me, that's a two way street, sweetheart."

For the second time in twenty-four hours, Asher walks out of my place leaving me hot and unsatisfied.

He turns in the doorway and pins me with a cocky look. "Oh, and I want a key to your place."

Chapter Thirteen

sher

I toss and turn all night. I can't stop thinking about Lotta's empty refrigerator. It doesn't fit the image I have of her–of the spoiled pack princess who gets everything she wants or needs handed to her on a silver platter.

Why would her pantry be bare? Why would she say she can't afford meat? She has a job. She has rich parents. She just graduated from an expensive private college.

But she's been denying her wolf for years. That came as a total shock. That level of self-denial... it says something about her. Who she is. The amount of self-control she must have. But also, of her inner conflict. There's a literal war going on inside her. Her wolf refused to stay sublimated when she got in the proximity of her mate. But she doesn't want a mate. She especially doesn't want me.

Not that I want her, either.

This new information adds to my misgiving about the tears she cried while I was fucking her. Maybe they weren't just about finding out her mate is one of her students. Or about getting nailed by a guy who hates her. Maybe they were a release from letting her wolf out.

Or–a prickle travels across my skin–maybe they were spawned from grief that she lost the battle with her wolf.

"That's fucked up," I mutter, throwing my legs out of bed long before dawn again.

I slip out of the townhouse and climb onto my Ducati. When I turned sixteen, I couldn't afford to buy a car, but Greg Lane, the owner of Wolf Ridge Body Shop, cut me a smoking deal on this baby. I bought it with money from working weekends for Mrs. Angelson at Sweet Treats.

I ride to the Circle K where Cole and Casey Muchmore's dad works. It's a twenty-four hour gas station and convenience store at the edge of town. The only place open in the middle of the night. I buy bread, milk, eggs, bacon and sandwich meat with the money I have from the last packet of cash my dad mailed me.

My mate needs protein. She needs sustenance. That primitive impulse to protect and provide for her won't be ignored until I'm sure she's been fed. I drive back home and jog up the wash to her place, respecting her rules about no one seeing me coming or going.

Hell, I don't want anyone to see us, either. The last thing I need is for her uppity parents to find out that the pack pariah has been touching their precious daughter. Fate knows her mom would falsify evidence of some new, heinous crime to get me permanently kicked out of Wolf Ridge.

I don't know why I try the door handle.

I'm disturbed to find it unlocked. Even more disturbed when my beautiful mate doesn't stir. I only hear the deep, even breath of heavy slumber from her. Either her wolf instincts for danger are dead, or she hasn't recovered her energy and stamina yet from the shift.

All the more reason for me to be here. I walk softly to her refrigerator and open the door. The light doesn't make her stir, either. I put the groceries inside and close it.

I should get back home and see if I can sleep another hour before school. Or head to the bakery to help my mom and Mrs. Angelson. Instead, I find myself standing over Lotta's bed, looking down at the lovely curve of her cheek. The curl of her dark lashes against her cheek.

I'm unnerved by a desire to crawl into bed with her. Hold her.

Fuck that. Boning her hard from behind is one thing. Cuddling is something I will never let happen. She doesn't deserve that from me. She's not someone I can trust.

Still, my fingers reach to caress her cheek the way I did yesterday in the school bathroom when she slapped my hand away. I stop myself before I actually touch her.

Why doesn't she wake up? She should know that some-one's broken into her house and is standing over her.

But then I realize–her wolf knows I'm safe.

Lotta the teacher may hate my guts. Lotta the artist. Lotta my neighbor. But her wolf isn't ever going to stop me. Her wolf knows I belong here.

That she belongs to me.

Our futures are woven together so tightly neither of us will ever be free.

* * *

Lotta

I sleep like the dead. Like I did the night of the full moon.

I guess that's what sex with my mate does to me. I have to sleep off the intensity. The extreme pleasure.

Fortunately, I don't sleep through my alarm, but I wake up with drool on my pillow and lines on my face from the pillowcase. I stumble to the bathroom and flick on the light.

The white shower curtain is standing up, disheveled from last night. I stoop to pick up a crumb from the grilled cheese sandwiches and remember how it felt to be cared for. Asher may act like a dick, but he's my mate. Taking care of me is what he's wired to do.

It's just biology, I tell myself fiercely when a warm flush spreads through my chest. *He hates you. There will be no claiming.*

I'd be foolish to believe he did anything last night out of caring for me.

No one cares for me–not truly. Not even my parents. I learned that the hard way when I didn't do what they wanted me to do. I made it just fine on my own at college. I had my art. Art is something that has never betrayed me. It's the friend I will always have.

Besides, even if Asher wasn't my student and the relationship completely forbidden, I don't *want* to be claimed. I don't want a relationship with Asher. I need to earn enough money to get back to Chicago, or if I can swing it–New York or Los Angeles. I need to be around other artists. Get my work out there and try to make it.

Nothing would be more sad than me getting claimed by some wolf from my high school and staying here the rest of my life. Giving up on all my dreams. Satisfying my parents' idea of a future for me.

"Ugh, no," I mutter as I turn on the water and step into the shower. I hold my head under the spray and try to forget how magnificent Asher looked naked. That glorious broad chest and shoulders. The light dusting of tawny curls over his tanned skin. He's incredible.

Sex with him is so different than it was with Andy–my college roommate–or even with the guys I hooked up with during the full moon runs in high school. He's crazy dominant, which turns me on. A little mean. Also, a turn-on. I might need to examine that. But even with the meanness, the growls and spanks, underneath it all, Asher is a considerate lover. He's completely in tune with me. Paced to my pleasure. He knows what I need and how to give it. If he denies me pleasure, that's purposeful, too.

It's night and day different from Andy's self-absorption or the intense but awkward and fumbled efforts of my teenage lovers.

Asher may be younger than I am, but he fucks like a man. A real man.

Oh Fate. I'm falling for him.

I *do not* want to fall for this guy.

I shampoo and condition my hair, shave my legs, underarms, and between my legs, and step out of the shower. My stomach growls as I dry off. Despite the three and half sandwiches I ate last night, I'm hungry again.

Crap. Asher probably used up the last of the bread and cheese for the grilled cheese sandwiches last night, which means there's nothing for my breakfast or to pack for lunch.

Maybe if I'm lucky, someone brought donuts to the staff room. Not that donuts are what Dr. Oakley recommended to nourish my wolf.

I exit the bathroom and get dressed then open the refrigerator door to see what I can scrounge.

"Oh!" I stare in shock at the food there. Milk. Eggs. Bread. Bacon. Sandwich meat.

Tears prick my eyes. I haven't felt this cared for since I graduated high school.

It's just biology, my logical brain insists. *He doesn't care.*

But this took thought. Asher came back in the middle of the night or while I was in the shower this morning. He had to get up early, go to the store, buy food, and bring it here. He does care.

Even angry. Even hating me for what I did, he still cares about my well-being.

My stomach growls again. I uncap the milk with shaky fingers and start guzzling it down, desperate for the calories and the protein. I start to look for scissors or a knife to open the package of bacon, and then my wolf takes over. I rip the stiff plastic open with my fingers. *Easily!* My shifter strength is returning.

There's no time to fry the bacon, so I press four pieces between several folded paper towels and microwave them while I fry four eggs in a pan and make a quick meat and cheese sandwich for lunch.

The whole time there's a warmth in my chest that won't go away.

Some of that heaviness that's been in my limbs for ages is gone. And it's not just about the wolf strength. It's emotional.

I tear up again. I haven't had that sense of connectedness in such a long time.

Humans aren't like pack. I had friends in college–lots. But I had to keep my guard up, I couldn't reveal my secret to anybody, and that made me shun close relationships. I stayed in groups. I didn't get tight with any one person.

That's probably why I chose such a self-involved guy as Andy as my fuck-boy in the first place. I needed someone who would never look too closely at me.

Artist-me slams a wall down on the emotion.

I can't get stuck in Wolf Ridge. Wolf life is not my future—I belong in the city *for my art*.

Wolf-me ignores all that. I grab the bacon from the microwave, crush it into the eggs, and eat straight from the skillet.

The whole time, there's a wag in my tail.

And since Andy crossed my mind, I decide to follow up on that gallery meeting. I shoot him a text.

> When are you coming? Any luck getting me a meeting?

He texts back,

> Next week. I got a pimp suite at a resort.
> Can't wait to see you in a bikini.

Oh. Ew. Ugh.

> Not happening

I text back.

> I'm seeing someone here.

I have to tell him I'm not available. Asher and I have an agreement. He's not my boyfriend, but we have an undeniable biological bond. Even if I was interested in screwing Andy—which I'm absolutely not—I can't mess with nature. Asher's wolf believes I belong to him, which means he would fight any other male to the death over me.

Andy:

> Whatevs. We were always free and easy.

Me:

> I said not happening. Can you get me an intro or not?

Andy:

> I don't know, I was thinking of a favors for favors kind of trade.

Me:

> Again—not an option.

Andy:

> Kidding, babe. I'll see what I can do.

Then,

> You see what you can do, too

followed by a bikini emoji.

Not cool. Ugh. Did he not read the part about me seeing someone? What an asshole. Well, I was stupid to pin any hopes on help from him. I should've figured he was just after sex.

I text Olive instead.

> Hey remember when you offered to visit galleries with me?

She responds immediately.

> Absolutely!

Pack sticks together. My eyes smart a little with the relief of having someone on my side. The contrast of her friendship compared with Andy is marked.

Me:

> Really? When would be a good time
> for you?

Olive:

> Wednesday nights the galleries stay open
> late for Art Walk. We could grab dinner and
> make some visits.

Me:

> Perfect! Does this coming Wednesday
> work for you?

Olive:

> Yep. It's in my calendar.

Awesome.

I send kiss emojis to Olive and head out the door right on time. I climb in my Mini–the one my parents bought for my sixteenth birthday that they refused to let me sell to pay for college tuition.

A motorcycle cuts me off as I try to turn into the staff parking lot and then pulls into the spot by the art room. My spot.

I know before his helmet comes off who's driving.

I find another place to park, grab my sandwich, and walk toward him. As I walk, I slide the key to my casita off the key ring.

The same familiar dread at seeing him is still there, but in equal or larger part is excitement.

Heat.

Desire.

"You should watch where you're going, Ms. James. You almost ran into me." His wicked smirk brings out his two deep dimples. He leans against the Ducati, arms folded over his massive chest.

I raise my voice in case any other teacher or student is around. "That's a staff parking spot, Asher. Move the bike."

"Yes, ma'am," he says, without moving.

"*Now.*" I'm right in his personal space now, dragging in his cedar and sexy man scent.

His nostrils flare and eyes glow green as he takes a slow pull of mine.

I drop my set of keys and look down without moving.

For a moment, I think my ploy isn't going to work. Asher's too committed to being a dick to follow along. He gives me a long, slightly disparaging look, but he eventually leans over to pick them up.

When he hands them to me, I swap the set with the key to my casita.

I get a blast of his power, but this time, instead of anger or rage, it's lust.

"Move the bike," I repeat, tossing my hair. "Thank you for the food," I murmur as I strut past him.

I feel his gaze on my back–or more likely my ass–for my entire walk into the school building. I turn to look back when I get to the door. Only then does he cast a mocking salute my way and throw a leg over the bike to move it to student parking.

I find my own version of a smirk playing on my lips as I step into the school.

Chapter Fourteen

sher

A I slip out to Lotta's place after football, dinner, and homework. The key to her apartment burned a hole in my pocket all day long, and sitting in her class was pure torture. She never looked at me–not once– but she blushed every time I got hard watching her strut around the classroom in her hip-hugging skirt and heeled sandals. She wore this fitted black crop top with a daisy over her tits that made me want to shred the shirt to ribbons and bury my face there.

Knowing that *she* knows she's mine–that she's admitted it, no matter how reluctantly– shifted things for me. I don't have that sense of fury toward her.

The old anger and sense of betrayal still sits like a stone at the pit of my stomach, but it only gives me a sense of misgiving now–not full-on rage.

I stop outside Lotta's door. Huh. I can tell she's not around. Her jasmine scent isn't there. But more than that–I just know. My wolf is already in sync with her. I try the key, anyway, just to be sure it works.

It does, but the place is empty. Her car isn't parked under the carport next to her parents' garage.

My wolf snarls at being denied. Is she doing this on purpose? Trying to take the reins back on our sexual encounters?

It doesn't fit, though. Lotta felt different today. Less closed off. Her murmured *thank you* over the food was warm, and she proactively got me the key to her place.

Is she with her parents? No, the car wasn't there, I remind myself.

Ah.

The image of her car still sitting in the parking lot when I left after football practice snaps into my mind. The night of the full moon, she'd shifted at school. She must stay there to paint.

It makes sense–the canvasses she uses are huge. They would take up half her one-room apartment here. Besides, sleeping with that scent of paint thinner would drive her wolf crazy.

And her wolf is already a little nuts.

I jog back up the wash and get on the Ducati. I drive to school, but hide the bike behind a dumpster and the back wall of the school. I can't risk someone seeing it while driving by.

Lotta's car is in the parking lot, and there's a light on in the art studio. Knowing the doors to the school will be locked, I stand under the windows. I pick up a pebble to toss at the glass to get her attention but then go still, staring.

Lotta stands with her back to me, facing a large canvas. On the canvas is a giant wolf's face.

My wolf's face. Black fur with white around the muzzle and the chest. Bright green eyes.

My teeth are bared in a ferocious snarl, hackles raised,

shoulders hunched like I'm about to pounce. Saliva–or maybe it's the serum I would use to mark her–drips from my teeth.

My body reacts to the painting like I've been hit by another linebacker. A fiery cannonball explodes in my center, causing the stone in my stomach to shift and roll. My wolf thrills that I'm in the forefront of her mind. That he's her muse.

"Whoa," I murmur out loud.

Lotta startles at the sound of my voice. The windows are cracked for ventilation, and she whirls.

"Asher."

I could live my whole life and not forget the sweetness of hearing her say my name. The breathless syllables seem to convey both thrill and nerves at finding me under the window.

She sets her paintbrush down. "I'll let you in."

I memorize those words, too, feeling there's a metaphor in them. I don't stop to question *why* I want her to let me in emotionally, when my heart is so firmly closed to her.

She's my mate. That's explanation enough.

I stay in the shadow of the building as I skirt around to the doors.

Lotta's breathless when she opens them. Her feet are bare, and there's a smear of paint on her wrist. Her honey-sweet scent assaults me, nearly making me drop to my knees to shove up that skirt of hers and press my tongue where she needs it most.

Instead, I pick her up, my forearm tucking under her ass to lift her hips above mine, so she's straddling my waist. I carry her down the hallway to the art room. "Your *never at school* rule's gonna get broken tonight," I growl.

"Oh."

No protest. She wants it, too.

"If you make me stalk you, I'm gonna eat what I catch."

"Mm." Her legs tighten around my waist, the scent of her arousal driving me mad. "I lost track of time," she says, squirming in my arms.

I absolutely love that she thinks she owes me an explanation. That she understands her tight little body belongs to me.

I *do* intend to own it in every way possible.

I slide a hand up under her shirt as I walk, my thumb slipping under her bra to strum her nipple.

She squeezes her legs again, and her butt muscles tighten with her excitement.

I take her into the art studio, straight to the table where I sit. The way she has the room sectioned off with her paintings, no one looking in from the outside would be able to see us, even with the lights on as they are.

"Asher." That breathless intonation again.

She's driving me insane. I sit her ass down at the edge of the table and pull her knees up. She drops back to her forearms, eyes glowing an electric blue.

"Wearing these little skirts to school is gonna get you fucked," I warn. "Hard." I tug her panties too hard, and the delicate satin and lace tear in half.

"Hey," she protests, but I'm not having any rebuke from her.

I lick my middle three fingers and slap her pussy with them.

Her eyes widen.

"That's right." I push her knees toward her shoulders. She lies back, abandoning her perch on her forearms. "This pussy is getting spanked tonight."

"Wh-wh..." Her lips work to form words, but she's

apparently unable to complete them. I don't know whether she was trying to ask *why* or *what,* but it doesn't matter. I answer with another spank. I cradle my hand under one of her knees to hold it wide and start spanking her beautiful pussy with my three fingers.

Obviously, there's no power behind the spanks. They don't hurt her. But she's startled by the sensation, and it gets her turned on fast. I slap her clit, getting it to swell and protrude. Her arousal drips down onto the table.

I'll be thinking about that in every class until graduation, guaranteed.

"This is what happens when you get me blue-balled." I deliver quick, light taps to her folds. She pants and mewls, her inner thighs starting to quake.

I hold both knees open and lower my face between her legs, hovering just above her sex. My mouth is open, my tongue poised to lick her, but I deliberately delay, letting her feel the heat of my breath.

She pushes back up on her elbows to look.

I extend my tongue slowly.

She starts to shake and shiver preemptively. Her body knows the pleasure I'm about to deliver. She's on the edge, maybe even ready to orgasm at the first brush of my tongue.

I lock gazes with her, still making her wait.

She holds her breath.

"Come for me, Carlotta," I murmur and flick her clit with the tip of my tongue.

That's it. One flick. I want to see if it's possible. If I can wind my mate up so tightly she goes off on my command.

"Aaah!" She cries out, reaching down to shove her own fingers inside her as she comes.

I only give her a few seconds to indulge, then I pick up her hips and spin her, dropping her onto her knees on the table. "Did you think your punishment was over, little wolf?"

She moans. She rests on one forearm, her fingers still between her legs, working out the last shivers of her orgasm. I let her self-pleasure as I spank her ass.

I don't hold back. She's a wolf–any pain she feels will be momentary, mixed up with sex and arousal. I turn her ass red, slapping one side, then the other, then right in the middle over her sweet pussy.

Then it's too much for me. I need to be inside her. This time I was prepared–I brought a condom. I yank it out of my pocket and rip it open. "Turn around," I order.

Lotta's eyes are glazed and unfocused as she shakily turns onto her back again. "It's okay," she says, seeing the condom. "I saw Dr. Oakley yesterday. I should be safe by now."

My wolf is enraged that he can't get her pregnant. I'm just thrilled I get to come inside her.

I grab her hips and yank them right up to the edge of the table where I stand. I shove down my shorts and push in.

It's even better this time. Every time is better with Lotta.

And I wanted her so badly I nearly weep to be inside. This is where I belong. Nestled between my mate's thighs. I slide my hand up her shirt to fondle her breast as I bump her ass. Her legs rest against my trunk, ankles dancing over my shoulders.

"Oh."

"Is that how you like it? You want me deep?" The dirty-talk just comes naturally.

"Yes," she moans. "Deeper."

Aw, fuck.

I grip the fronts of her thighs to hold her steady and drill in, making her take all of me, as deep as I can get it. The room spins. I want it to last forever, but I'm already too far gone to hold out much longer.

It doesn't matter. Lotta's clearly in the throes herself. Her eyes are rolling back in her head, chin arced up toward the ceiling in ecstasy.

"Are you going to come when you're told?" I ask.

Her eyes try unsuccessfully to focus on mine.

"Hmm? Are you going to be a good girl and come when I tell you?"

"I...I..." She's clearly incapable of speech now.

I already know she will. This body was built to submit to mine. Just like mine was built to serve hers.

Making her scream in pleasure isn't just my right. It's my destiny.

I find her nipple and pinch it, slowly tightening my hold until she squirms.

My balls draw up. I'm feverish and hot. "Now, Lotta," I growl and shove in deep. My balls tighten and pump sending streams of hot cum into her.

I release my hold on Lotta's nipple and give the side of her breast a light slap.

She comes, her slender hips bucking against mine, her slick juices mixing with my essence.

I slide my hand over her breast in more of a caress. I squeeze lightly, then stroke down her side to her waist.

She looks magnificent. Her raven hair spreads in a halo around her head. Her eyes are closed, berry lips parted in an "O" as she squeezes and milks my cock for more.

"That's right," I encourage, bumping my loins against her ass in short beats. "Take it all. Every last drop."

She moans and hooks her ankles behind my back,

pulling me in tight against her to grind out the last of her orgasm.

* * *

Lotta

There is nothing in the world like sex with Asher.

I had no idea it could get this good. And I have a feeling we're just getting started.

It seems I'm helpless against refusing him. I vowed never to have sex with Asher at school again, yet, here I am, splayed out on one of my classroom's tables with my panties torn to shreds on the floor.

As my brain returns, so do my misgivings about what we're doing. About my inability to stop myself. About my feelings for Asher.

Because the fact is, I do have feelings.

I cared deeply for him when he was thirteen. Maybe my wolf knew him on some level, even without the presence of his wolf. What I feel now is that caring tangled with a hurricane of dangerous desire. And the more concerned I feel for him, the more pressure I feel to flee. To leave Wolf Ridge before it's too late. Before I'm locked into something with him that I can never be free of.

I look away as I unlock my ankles from behind his back and use my feet on his thighs to push him away. Out of my peripheral vision, I see his upper lip curl into a snarl, but he accepts my abrupt change of heart. He walks to the sink and washes up as I slide off the table. I clean up with a few tissues from the tissue box, which I put in my purse to dispose of in the toilet later. Leaving any evidence of our tryst in the classroom would be disastrous.

Asher picks up my panties and pockets them. He saunters over to my studio area and stands with his arms folded, taking in the painting I'm working on.

"When did you start this one?"

"In August."

He looks over, brows jumping in surprise.

"What? It takes a long time to complete a painting this size."

"You hadn't seen my wolf in August."

I blink, not understanding. Then I stare at the wolf on the canvas and gasp, my hand clapping over my mouth.

It *is* Asher.

Why did I not put that together? In addition to painting my wolf, I've been painting variations of this giant black wolf since my sophomore year of college.

Since Asher would have transitioned to his wolf form.

I sway on my feet.

Asher circles an arm around my waist and pulls me up against his firm body. "They're all of us," he murmurs with awe in his voice. I scan all the paintings, large and small, stacked against the walls or on easels to see what he sees.

Fate, how did I miss it? Every painting features either a giant black male wolf or a slender white she-wolf, both with green eyes. I thought of them as yin and yang. To me, they represented the male and female wolf aspects. Sometimes I painted them together. Mostly apart. Sometimes I painted my face superimposed with my wolf's or with the wolf's face over my chest area.

I *never, ever dreamed I was painting a specific male.*

I never attached a human face to Asher's wolf. Never imagined what that particular male looked like in human form.

How utterly bizarre that I didn't note their similarities the first time I saw Asher on the full moon run. Even when

I caught his cedar and soap scent and suspected he was my mate, I didn't make the connection. I'm so out of touch with my wolf nature, I missed all the clues Fate was dropping for me.

"So you suppressed your wolf at art school, and this is how she emerged." Asher's voice is a comforting tumble above my head.

I don't want to lean back against his sturdy support because it feels too good. I don't want to get used to something I don't get to keep. My body doesn't obey my wishes. I'm melting into him, drinking in how marvelous it feels to have the corded muscles of his forearm holding me up.

"Yes. She became my artistic muse."

Asher releases me and walks closer to examine a 48 x 48-inch painting of my wolf standing in a mountain meadow surrounded by delicate gold Mexican poppies. I had this painting in my bedroom in the dorm-style apartment I shared with Andy and two other seniors last year. Having her close kept me from feeling like I would go crazy.

"She looks..." He tilts his head, as if he's trying to read the mind of my wolf on the canvas. "I think she's mad at you."

A choked sort of laugh comes out of my mouth. "Mad?" I walk to his side.

"Don't you see it?"

"Well...I would've said she looks wise. Or strong." I, too, tilt my head and try to see her through Asher's eyes.

"Maybe she is mad."

"She looks bitter."

"I might call it repressed."

"The repression made her bitter."

That gnawing guilt I have over suppressing my wolf comes to the surface. I elbow him. "Don't judge."

Asher picks me up and sits me atop the step ladder I use to paint the upper region of the canvas. I don't see any of that resentment or rage he usually holds for me. Nor do I see the condemnation of my parents. His face is relaxed–his expression soft. When his hands come to rest lightly on the sides of my thighs, a trembling starts in the center of my being.

"It just seems like a...violence you enacted on yourself."

I want to react with the habitual defensiveness I reserved for every conversation I had with my parents while I was in school, but Asher's thumbs lightly stroke the tops of my thighs, and I can't concentrate.

"What made you do it?"

I sweep my arm to indicate the paintings. "Art, Asher."

His brows furrow. "You suppressed your wolf, so you could paint her?"

My laugh is bitter. "No. But I couldn't have both. I chose art."

Asher stares at me so long with a look of confusion that I start to question my own premise.

"My parents say shifters don't care about art. They wanted me to stay and work at the brewery, like everyone else."

A look of scorn flits over Asher's face, and I want to hug him. "That's...really dumb."

"All the best art schools and art scenes are in major cities. Places where a wolf can't shift and run. I applied to the Art Institute of Chicago, anyway, and I was lucky enough to be accepted."

"Oka-ay." Asher draws the word out, implying he still doesn't get it.

"My parents forbade me from going. They said it would

kill my wolf, but I was an adult. I pretty much gave them the middle finger and went anyway."

Understanding dawns on Asher's face. "They wouldn't pay. That's why you can't afford to keep meat in the house."

Tears spring to my eyes, and I blink them back. After hiding so much of who I was at college and feeling so caged, it feels incredible to be seen. Understood.

"I have student loans to pay off, and I couldn't find a job that paid enough to cover rent in Chicago. Basically, my parents starved me out as punishment for disobeying them. My mom lured me back with this temporary art job, but when she figured out I was planning on using it to get back on my feet and return to the city, she informed me that I have to pay rent to stay in their casita."

"What? That's fucked up."

"So I have no hope of paying down the loans. I'm just saving everything I earn to try to get started somewhere else."

Asher glances toward the windows, as if realizing for the first time that we might be seen together, and lifts me down from the stepladder. "Well, I'm glad you have your art."

He picks up a small six inch by six inch painting of our two wolves and studies it then walks away with it in his hand.

"What are you doing? You can't take that!"

Asher turns and gives me a slow smirk. I hate what his dimples do to my insides.

"Oh, I'm taking, sweetheart. Or are you gonna make me give it back?" He waggles it in the air as if to tempt me.

I have no idea why his taunt makes me wet. Maybe just his call-out to our size and power difference. To the fact that he can do whatever he wants with me, whenever he chooses, and I won't stop him because I crave it.

I should be mad at his disrespect, but instead, a ribbon of warmth that streaks through me.

Asher wants my art. It does have some value to a shifter.

More than that, it means something to him.

"Unlock your phone, Ms. James." He's been in my purse, apparently, because he has my phone. He flashes it up to my face, and the phone unlocks.

"I'm putting my number in here." His thumbs move over the screen. "If you want me to take care of your needs, you'd better tell me where you're gonna be."

"I'm sorry. I will." I screw up my courage as I walk over to him on the other side of the canvases. "Asher." I owe him a bigger apology. The explanation I'll hold back, but an apology is a start. "I just want to say that I'm sorry about what happened with your da–"

"Don't." The blast of cold from Asher is palpable. His upper lip curls into a snarl.

Even knowing he's my mate and should be incapable of harming me, I take a step back. His power is intimidating.

"I'm putting that shit aside to take care of your wolf's needs. If you open that box"–he shakes his head– "You don't want to see me when I get mean."

Chapter Fifteen

sher

A I lie in my bed holding Lotta's painting of our wolves standing in a meadow in one hand. In my other, I finger the little gold moon pendant I stole from her when I was thirteen.

I just returned from her place where we had a frenzied, wordless fuck over her kitchen table followed by a second, silent round that featured her face down on the bed, where I held her down by her nape as I took her slowly for as long as I needed.

I've been a dick to Lotta since she tried to apologize last week about my dad. I've kept up my end of the bargain–slipping over there after dark and satisfying her. I've given it to her rough. Avoided conversation.

I can't seem to help myself. When his memory gets invoked, I become a version of him. I turn into that violent troublemaker everyone in this damn pack expects to see when they look at me.

I got written off by teachers and pack elders by third grade. Like my dad, I struggled with my temper. The violence at home transferred to violence at school. I was already getting into trouble for fights in elementary school. I threw my book at a teacher for scolding Seb for something he hadn't done. I held a kid upside down by his ankles until he apologized for pulling Casey Muchmore's hair.

Everyone assumed I would become a little hoodlum, so I met their expectations. My teachers hated me, so I hated them. Or who's to say which came first? Regardless, that's why I was doing so poorly in school at the time Lotta made me her tutoring project. The school had put my name on a referral list for volunteer tutors, and she chose me.

She met with me three times a week. It took me a while to believe that she really wanted to help, but she persisted.

I wouldn't say she was the first person who cared about me because my mom cared. My dad cared in his own way. Mrs. Angelson cared.

Lotta saw my potential where others saw rebellion. She was invested in my success. Of course, it didn't hurt that she was beautiful. Sometimes it was hard to focus on her lessons because I was mesmerized by the shape of her bowtie lips as she spoke. By the jade glow of her eyes. But eventually, I repaid her attention by actually applying myself to my work, and she brought me from failing to As and Bs by the end of the semester.

Tonight when I slapped her ass and walked out the door, she said, "I'm expecting you to turn in that self-portrait, Asher. Don't make me fail you."

Part of me wanted to turn around and tell her to give me an A, or I'd tell the whole school we're fucking, but I couldn't. And the reason isn't all based on honor.

It also seems to have something to do with this little painting of us.

The canvas does something to me. It produces a sense of

fullness in my chest. A yearning. Maybe that's the effect of art.

I can't believe Lotta's parents told her there's no place for art in a pack. What are we, heathens? We can't appreciate beauty or art? We just run around and eat, fuck, and reproduce and stay in our tightly-knit pack full of assholes? I don't get it.

But I never did understand this life we lead here. I've always chafed against authority, against what they want me to do, against everything Wolf Ridge stands for.

I study all the detail she worked into such a tiny canvas. The background is familiar. She didn't make it up. She must've painted by memory.

I realize I know the meadow in the painting. It's an incredible hollow up in the mountains. Surrounded in all directions by tree-lined mountainsides, it's a gorgeous open field that fills with wildflowers in the spring. It's the perfect place to pitch a tent and camp. Or to paint. If I remember right, it's far–a solid hour and a half run on four legs. And the only road that goes to it is an old bumpy Jeep trail–not fit for a car. I could get there on my motorcycle, though.

Something about this homage to me, or to our wolves, makes me actually want to do the assignment. Despite the fact that I shut down all communication, I still have this desire to express myself to her. To show what I am.

And it's not the person I pretend to be. I'm not just the hell-raiser who will probably turn out to be a criminal like his father. The man who stole from the pack. But I did steal this necklace from the beautiful girl up the road.

I am also the guy who kept it all these years, bitter over her betrayal yet still obsessed. Still hoping there was some explanation for why she hurt me the way she did. Why she used what I told her in confidence against me and my family when she promised she wouldn't.

My mom taps on my door and comes in. "Hey, honey." There's a frown between her brows. "I heard something today."

I groan and sit up. This is the drawback of small towns and wolf packs. Moms hear things. Nothing is ever private.

I brace, instinctively knowing it's going to be about Lotta.

She folds her arms over her chest. "I heard the fight you were in happened in Lotta James' classroom. That she's teaching art at the school now."

Fuck. I rub my face. Guilt twists in my gut. My mom doesn't know I'm the one who told Lotta about Dad stealing money from the pack, but she knows Lotta's mom is on the council and was responsible for getting him banished.

I know my mom feels ashamed of Dad and avoids the council members or ducks her head in submission when she sees them. I fucking hate it.

"Yeah," I admit.

"You didn't even tell me you had her as a teacher, and now I find out she's the reason you got suspended?"

Fuck.

"She's..." My brain goes blank. I can't trust myself to say anything about Lotta that won't reveal too much. I settle for, "I got myself suspended. It was just in her class, Mom."

She continues to consider me with concern. "You should be careful around her, Asher. You know her mom's on the council. If she thinks for one second that you're a danger to her daughter, you'll be out of here."

"I'm not a danger to her daughter," I grumble. Guilt seeps from my pores.

"Well, I know that, but you just got suspended for

breaking a kid's wrist in her class. That doesn't look good, does it?"

"I know. I–" I sigh and stand. "I'll be more careful, Mom." I lean down to kiss her forehead. "I'm sorry, Mom."

She gives me a hug and leaves, and I drop my head to the door. Dammit. This is a prime reason why I can never claim Lotta James.

It would break my poor mother's heart.

* * *

Lotta

A text comes in from Andy between classes. He sent flowers to my house yesterday. I promptly brought them over to my mom's house and opened the windows at my place to air out the smell. The last thing I need is for Asher's wolf to get triggered thinking some other male is sniffing in his territory.

I also texted Andy last night to say,

> I told you I'm seeing someone. If the gallery intro is hinging on us hooking up, then I don't want your intro.

He responds now.
Andy:

> babe, it's all cool, you know you're still my girl.

Me:

> ?No, I just told you I'm seeing someone.

Andy:

Don't be like that. I'll be there this week.
We'll meet up and talk.

Me:

Forget it. I'm not interested.

This is getting stupid. He didn't pay this much attention to me when we were living together. Why is he acting stalker-y now?

Asher and his baller buddies walk in the classroom as the bell rings, and I shove my phone back in my purse and start taking attendance.

When I'm finished, I say, "I should have a paragraph from every one of you by now describing what form your self-portrait will be," I announce in sixth period.

I fan myself with a folder I grab from my desk. I'm having a hot flash. It started the moment Asher walked in the classroom and hasn't let up.

Worse than the heat is the steady pulse between my legs.

I'm in a room full of shifters. Literally all of them will be able to smell my arousal if they're paying attention. I need to get a grip on this.

"Asher, I don't have one for you. If you want to play in the next game, you need to come and see me right now. The rest of you may work on your projects."

My stomach tightens as Asher unfolds from his chair and saunters up to the front of the class.

I hold my head high despite the wave of dizziness that comes over me when he gets close. I can barely breathe—the air feels too thick and charged.

As arranged, he's been taking care of my needs.

Showing up after dark and letting himself into my casita with the key I gave him. But he's been cold. Angry. Every encounter leaves me simultaneously satisfied and empty.

Today, I feel a pressure I haven't felt before. It's a biological pressure, I think, at least, it's coming from my wolf. But not to have sex.

To soothe my mate? To connect with him?

I don't know. All I know is everything feels terribly wrong, and I can barely think.

I hold my ground, even when Asher gets too close, crowding into my space and towering over me, so I have to tilt my head way back to look in his eyes.

I hope he won't call my bluff on benching him. I simply don't want to go toe-to-toe with him. He's angry with me. He's holding a grudge.

One I well deserve.

He's acting out, like the rebellious bad boy he's always been.

That's not the side of him I want to bring out, and drawing a line in the sand is just going to continue this dilemma.

"I will waive the written paragraph requirement if you can verbalize to me now what your plan is for the self-portrait."

Asher's brows pop. He shoves his hands in the pockets of his worn jeans and looks out the window.

"If you don't have any ideas, I'd like to help you figure something out."

He drags his gaze back to mine. "No, I have an idea." A thoughtful gleam is in his seagreen eyes.

It's my turn to be surprised. "Okay. What is it?"

"Multimedia project. A collage, I guess. With other stuff, too."

At first, I think he's just blowing smoke up my ass and really has no idea or plan, but then he says, "I need one of those little canvases." He holds his hands in the shape of a square the size of the little painting of us that he stole from me.

Oh. Damn. Does that mean something?

No, probably not. I'm reading too much into it. But it's getting hard to stand up straight with him so close. I sway on my feet.

I hate this loss of control. I hate trying to navigate a relationship with my most difficult student when all I can think about is tearing his clothes off. All I want is to feel his hands on me.

I'm shaking now.

"Okay. Great," I hope I sound as bright as I'm trying to sound.

I circle around behind my large canvases to find a stretched four-inch frame for him. Of course, he follows me.

When I turn to hand it to him, he's right there.

I blink back my tears of frustration. Not with him. Not with the situation. I can handle all of this. What I can't handle is this complete loss of control over my own body. The way my wolf is pushing through and making me feel like I'm going to split in two.

Asher catches me by the nape. His large hand holds me steady, but instead of bringing relief, his support just makes me want to cry even more. I blink hard against the rush of tears.

This isn't a person I can rely on.

I may want to trust him, and he may be physically safe for me, but I'm not emotionally safe with this guy. Not even remotely.

I'm still alone, still a fish out of water, just like in college only now reversed.

Asher's brows slam down. He doesn't take the canvas from me, but instead cradles my face with both hands.

A tear streaks my cheek.

He thumbs it away and shakes his head slowly in a silent soothing.

I want to pull away, but I'm incapable. It feels too good to be touched by him. Every place he's in contact with, my skin feels electrified. I drink in his essence.

He drags me closer and presses his lips silently to the top of my head. "It's okay." He barely breathes the words against my hair. No one would hear it.

His gaze flicks toward the window.

I whirl, but no one is out there. He was just keeping watch for us. For me.

I'm the one who would suffer if we were caught.

"Thanks," he says in a normal voice, taking the canvas from my shaking fingers.

My head wobbles as I try to say "sure." I clear my throat. "Let me know if you need anything else."

"Oh, I *will* need more." It sounds like a threat.

My pussy contracts. I'm lightheaded again. I walk quickly away, careening a bit like a drunken sailor, then righting myself.

I don't know how I'm going to make it through the rest of the semester. If I were smart, I would pack up and leave town right now.

Screw the job.

Except I already see the brick wall I'm speeding toward. A huge, horrible crash is inevitable for me. And I don't even know which of the looming walls on all sides I hope to hit. All I can wish for is that it doesn't destroy me entirely.

Chapter Sixteen

sher

Once more, I'm shaken by Lotta's tears, and my teammates take the brunt of it.

Coach Jamison blows the whistle at me when I knock Seb ten feet into the air.

Why was she crying? Last time I was sure it wasn't something I'd done. I gave her what she needed, she just didn't *want* to need it.

This time, though, a terrible niggling feeling tells me it's because I've been a bastard to her. Is it possible she does care how I feel about her?

That it hurts her when I'm cruel?

I somehow thought the tiny half-pint of authority didn't give a fuck about me or the fact that I hate her. I thought she didn't give a fuck about what she'd done because she left town without an explanation. She stayed away for over four years.

Here I've been relentlessly punishing her and not believing it had any effect.

Seb is usually laid-back, but he doesn't appreciate

landing on his back from such a height. He jumps up with a growl and tries to tackle me. I plow into him at the same time, and our bodies collide with a loud crack.

"Dude, what's your problem?"

I roll my shoulders under the pads and snap my head to make my neck crack. "Nothing. Sorry, man."

After practice, I shower. Knowing Lotta's in the building makes showering with the guys insufferable. I have to force myself not to think of her. Not to remember that she's close by. That I could easily pick up that tight little body of hers, pin her against a wall, and show her how much agony she puts me in.

Today, the thought of those tears keeps me from getting a hard-on while I shower.

Remembering the salty scent agitates me. The need to fix whatever is bothering her eats at me.

I take my time toweling off and packing up my bag to leave. Then I sit and pull out my phone, staring at the screen, trying to formulate a plan.

"You need to talk, Asher?" Coach Jamison startles me from my reverie. He's leaning against the lockers, looking at me.

"Oh, uh, no Coach."

"She-wolf problems?"

"Ah, not really. Well, yeah. Kind of."

Coach grins. "Which is it?"

"I don't know. They're confusing, right?"

He chuckles. "They are certainly more complicated than we are. Sounds like you need a date night. To connect with your girl away from school and pack, so you can get to know each other as people. Have you done that yet?"

I try to push the image of me banging Lotta on all fours in the middle of that king-sized bed of hers last night.

"Uh no. That's a good idea, Coach."

I stand and sling my bag over my shoulder and look back at the screen of my phone. Maybe Coach is right. A conventional date isn't possible, but changing things up couldn't be a bad thing. An idea starts to form in my mind as I walk out of the building, and I send a text to Lotta.

> Meet me at the old blinking light at six. I'll bring dinner.

* * *

Lotta

The "old blinking light" is now actually a regular stoplight, but it used to be a blinking red light at the crossroads between town and the mountain passes. A four-way stop sign between highways.

There's an abandoned building that once housed a diner that someone should tear down. But there are a lot of things in Wolf Ridge that haven't changed in the hundred and twenty years since wolf shifters settled here, a lot of things that need an update.

I pull up and park behind the abandoned building, so my car is hidden from the roads.

It's a strange place to meet, and I don't know what Asher has in mind, but I am actually grateful he's demanding we break the rules I set up for us. I may need his touch every night, but I don't know if I could take another cold "servicing" after dark at my place.

I keep replaying that kiss on the top of my head in the classroom today. Of all the things Asher's done to me, it seems like an unlikely one to latch onto, but it hit a tender spot.

A needy spot.

It wasn't sexy. Or rough. Or dominant.

It wasn't angry or cold.

There was a caring and compassion to it that registered in my body like the scrape of a match against flint. It ignited something different than passion.

Yikes.

Intimacy?

My heart rate picks up, and my palms get sweaty. I throw the door to my car open and climb out to ease the restlessness of my wolf. Was she the one who wants intimacy or does she just need the sex? I tend to think of my wolf side as purely physical. As the not-thinking side. The biological urge side.

So maybe it's me, the lonely artist, who craves connection.

That thought twists and snags like knotted yarn. Confusion blankets me like a deep fog. I thought it had it all worked out--deny my wolf to pursue art.

When being near my fated mate made that impossible, I hoped to deny an emotional connection, so I wouldn't get stuck here in Wolf Ridge, pregnant at twenty-two, giving up on my dreams.

But I don't know what to do with the longing that Asher inspired that isn't sexual.

I don't know what to do with all my carefully laid-out plans that he's smashing to smithereens.

I detect the sound of a motorcycle approaching and hush the burst of pleasure that explodes in my body. The dopamine rush of knowing I'm about to see him.

Knowing I'm certainly going to get well-laid tonight. Asher always takes care of my needs.

I attempt to still my heart when he pulls up wearing a

pair of wrap-around sunglasses, his muscles bulging beneath a fitted t-shirt. He's not wearing a helmet, which is only a state law if you're under eighteen in Arizona. It's not necessary for a shifter although a bad enough accident involving a skull fracture could certainly kill us.

I shove my worry for Asher out of my mind. He's strong and healthy. Alpha through and through. Nothing's going to happen to him. Why does thinking about him being in an accident make me lose my breath? Why am I already sure my heart would smash into smithereens if he wasn't okay?

He pulls up but doesn't shut the bike off. Instead, he jerks his head, beckoning me over.

I look around, to see if any cars are coming down the highways.

"I won't let anybody see you with me." Fate—when did I fall in love with his deep growly voice? "Promise."

I try to tamp down that flutter of excitement taking wing in my belly. This isn't romance. We're not on a date.

He's my student.

Student.

This is illegal.

For some reason, that thought only makes it more exciting. I've been the quiet artist my entire life. With a wolf that is small in stature, I bowed to the alpha nature of all my classmates but differentiated myself by following my passion. My mom's high status in the pack ensured I was never picked on and still included with the royal clique.

Now it seems, I'm going to be the bad girl.

I throw a leg over Asher's motorcycle and settle onto the seat behind him. I'm in a skirt and flip flops—not the best motorcycling attire.

Asher immediately puts the bike in gear and takes off, making my hands fly to his middle to hold myself on.

And, oh *wow*. The ridges of his muscles stand out below my fingers. I can't stop myself from sliding my hands beneath his shirt to feel them skin-to-skin. His belly shudders when I do, showing me he's as affected by the intimate contact as I am. I stroke my hands up and down the contours of his six-pack.

My panties get wet. As Asher steers the motorcycle in the direction of National Forest land, I let my hands drop to his hips, then grip the tops of his thighs. I slide my palms up and down his thighs, dragging them up the inside until I find the bulge of his cock. His bike swerves when I stroke the length where it lies against his left thigh, making it grow and stretch. His belly shudders again.

He picks up speed, turning onto a dirt road that has clearly not been maintained. Only a four-wheel Jeep or motorcycle could drive on this road. I have to cling onto Asher's middle again as the ride gets rough. My muscles are taut, the muscles of my neck and abdomen tense, bracing against the bumps and swerves. I peer around Asher's shoulder to see what's coming next.

And then there comes a point when I surrender. I stop bracing for every climb and fall of the bike over the deep grooves in the road. Stop trying to control or manage my ride. Instead, I meld my torso to Asher's, lean my cheek against his back, and loosen my grip.

Pleasure rushes in. The thrill of the ride surrounds me. I close my eyes and take in the delicious smell of Ponderosa pine and sunbaked boulders. I drink in the scent of my mate–the warm cedar and soap. A faint whiff of fresh-baked bread. That masculine scent distinct to only him.

We ride for half an hour down the rugged road. I have no idea where he's bringing me. What he's planning.

Suddenly, the forest road opens into a gorgeous

meadow—a valley tucked into the mountains. Asher eases off the accelerator, gradually slowing to a stop. He leans the bike to the rest on its kickstand, twisting to catch me around the waist to ease my descent. I dismount and drink in the beauty of our surroundings, turning in a full 360.

Only then do I turn my gaze on Asher to try to discern what we're doing here.

"Run, Lotta," he says softly.

I blink, not understanding. His words didn't match his tone, so it takes a moment to assimilate the meaning. "What?"

His lips twitch. "You heard me, sweetheart. *Run.*"

* * *

Asher

Lotta kicks off her flip flops at the same time she whips her cute-as-fuck crop top off.

I slowly unbuckle my belt, my gaze glued to her tight little body.

Her exhilaration shows in the spark in her bright blue eyes, the speed at which she undresses. She heard the taunt in my voice, but she knows this is a game.

She drops her skirt and panties then unhooks her bra. Her nipples are taut, extended out in firm points. But I don't get to oggle them because in a flash, she drops to all fours, a blur of white fur as she takes off away from me.

I give her a head start. My wolf is bigger.

Much faster.

Plus, I relish the hunt. Crave the chase.

If it was too easy to catch her, the payoff wouldn't be as delicious. I take my time undressing, now deliberately not following her movements. I pick up her clothes and mine and drape them over the seat of my bike, then take out the cushy comforter I stuffed into one saddle bag and spread it out on a choice spot in the meadow. From the other saddle-bag, I retrieve the bag I packed with picnic food–meat, cheese, fruit, nuts, and wine. It's not that hard to convince the grocery clerk to sell you wine when you're both shifters. He knows I metabolize way too fast to ever be impaired by a bottle of wine.

The sun is setting, bathing the mountainsides in oranges and gold. I shift, trotting off in the direction she disappeared, my nose to the ground to follow her delectable scent. I catch it easily and pick up speed, the joy of running as my wolf mingling with the insatiable need to hunt, catch, and devour Carlotta James.

I run harder, instinct taking over, but then lose her scent.

My tricky mate.

She doubled back somewhere. I skid to a stop, pivot, and follow the trail back. It takes me a few minutes to figure out that she took a flying leap from one of the boulders to the earth below, but I pick up the scent again and charge forward.

I race forward, my paws digging into the soft earth as I climb in elevation. I catch sight of a flash of white fur in the trees and veer on the diagonal to cut her off. I don't mean to catch her, but I leap and end up pinning her beneath two paws.

She rolls under, baring her belly and throat to me. Submitting to me, her mate. Making me desperate to shift back and fuck her blind.

But I want her to enjoy the blanket I set up, so I release her, giving her a light nip to drive her back down the mountain. I chase, nip, and herd her down to the meadow, enjoying the way she slows to take in our picnic site then races for it.

My wolf goes insane with need for her.

We reach the blanket in seconds, both of us shifting to human form before we're down.

Mine, my wolf roars.

I ignore the fact that it's not true, dragging her closer by her legs, flipping her to her back, and spreading her wide. I lick into her at the same time I pinch both of her nipples.

She cries out in shock then moans her assent. I delve my tongue between her soft folds, exploring aggressively, fucking her with my tongue, sucking her labia into my mouth.

There's nothing nuanced about eating her. I'm consuming my mate like she's my last meal. Like if I don't make her come in the next instant, our lives will be over.

Her hips writhe and wiggle, legs squeeze around my shoulders. I continue to pinch and pull at her nipples, rolling them between my fingers, then squeezing her breasts roughly.

"Asher, please."

I love it when she begs.

"Please, I can't take it."

I stop sucking her clit and lift my head. "You can and you will." I flick my tongue over the swollen nub.

She whimpers. "*Please,* Asher. I need you inside me."

"You will come on my tongue first. Then you'll come all over my dick. Then I'm going to come in your ass."

That's all it takes–my beautiful mate comes from my words alone. Her ass squeezes tight, and her hips jack off the bedspread, thrusting her dripping cunt against my face. I cradle her ass in my hands and put my entire mouth over her, sucking as her muscles squeeze and pulse against my tongue.

"That's it, baby," I murmur between licks. "You taste so sweet when you come all over my tongue."

Lotta goes feral, sitting up and tackling me to my back. She straddles my waist and catches my sizable erection. I groan at the contact, my balls already drawing up to come.

But I force myself to relax. I want more than a frenzied fuck tonight.

I want Lotta.

All of her.

She lifts her hips up and lowers herself onto my cock, eyes rolling up in her head with a moan.

I take her hips but don't guide her yet. I want to feel her gyrations. Learn the dance she does when I let her follow her own pleasure.

She settles, taking me even deeper, panting. Her eyes glow green. She's so exquisite, with her dark, thick hair cascading over her shoulders, the curve of her cheekbones set off by the flush of color in her face.

One rock of her hips, and my cock surges even longer.

I tighten my grip on her hips but still don't take over. I let her savor the control, seek her pleasure. Her hands drop to my shoulders, her long hair tickling my chest. She slides forward and back over my root. She's slick as fuck, her juices leaking down my balls.

"Show me how well you ride my cock," I growl.

Her nails score my skin as she picks up speed. She finds an internal ridge she likes the head of my cock to rub against and grinds there. Her short, quick strokes wind the coil of sexual tension tighter and tighter, but I force myself to hold off.

I have plans for her ass tonight. I force air in through my nostrils and exhale through my teeth.

"Come on my cock, baby. Show me how much you like to ride it."

Lotta's moan has a wild timbre. I distract myself from the need building in my balls by watching Lotta's pleasure grow and bloom.

She loses herself, throwing her head and tits to the sky and shifting her grip to my thighs behind her. She's a goddess, breasts bouncing, back arching, as she rocks forward and back over my cock.

Her breath grows frantic. She switches her grip back to my chest, taking me deep as she gyrates over my dick.

I lick the pad of my thumb. "Go ahead. Show me how you grip my cock when you come." I bring my thumb to her clit and press.

She convulses with pleasure, her inner thighs squeezing around my hips, her internal muscles contracting and pulsing.

I don't know how I manage not to come. Stars dance before my eyes. My teeth grind. The urge to mark Lotta is so strong it's a wonder I don't flip her to her back and sink my teeth into her shoulder. Forever mark her with my scent. Take her freedom as my due.

But I force myself not to move until I regain control. Only then do I roll our bodies to flip on top. I'm about to pull out and tell her to roll over when I catch a trace of fear and vulnerability in her expression.

In my mind, she's on top. She's still my tutor, and I'm the infatuated student. She's my teacher. The girl who wrecked me once. I forget that I have the power to hurt her —not just physically but emotionally too.

She was crying today in her classroom over us. I brought her here to make it up to her.

"Good girl," I praise her obedience. I catch her jaw in my hand and kiss her, mating my mouth to hers, my tongue sweeping into her mouth. It's a demanding kiss, but not violent like our first one. Our only other one.

My hips rock, the steely length of my aching cock sliding through her juices

I realize it's a necessary kiss, one I didn't know I so desperately needed. I slow down and explore her lips with mine. They're soft–infinitely soft–and after a moment, she begins to kiss me back.

"You're beautiful." I stroke her hair back from her face.

Her eyes are blue again, staring up at me with that touch of vulnerability still. Like she doesn't want to care about me or what I think about her, but she does.

"Beautiful. And mine." I kiss her again before she can rebel at that statement. This time, I make love to her mouth. Stroke my lips over hers, changing angles, tasting her. I kiss and nibble down her neck, pull out to crawl lower and swirl my tongue around her left nipple.

She moans softly. It's a sound I could get used to for the rest of my life. And for the first time, I consider what that life might look like.

I told Abe I would never claim Lotta. It's not true.

The truth is, I would claim her in a heartbeat if I thought she wanted me back. I would claim her, and I would do everything it took to make her happy.

I gently roll her to her belly and reach for the bag I packed with our picnic goodies. There's a bottle of lubricant in there that I plan to use.

I slide my fingers between her legs and stroke over her

soaked slit with one hand, as I uncap the lube with the other.

I hold her ass cheeks apart and squeeze some lube over her back hole, then massage it around that tight rosebud.

Latta writhes over the comforter.

"Are you gonna take it in the ass like a good girl?" I penetrate her back hole with one of my fingers, gently stretching and preparing it to make room for my cock.

Lotta looks over her shoulder at me. The slight alarm in her expression tells me she's an anal virgin.

I lean forward and kiss her shoulder, reassuring her. "I'll make it good for you," I promise. "Do you believe that?"

Her lids droop, and she nods.

"I know what your body needs, don't I, baby?" My fingers penetrate her juicy sex as my thumb stretches her back hole.

She moans.

"You want more?" I'm never one to force myself on a female, mate or not. I may be dominant, but I'm not an asshole.

She hesitates, clearly still a little nervous, but I have her hips writhing. "Yes."

"Say it. Say, *please fuck me in the ass, Asher.*"

Her cunt squeezes around my fingers.

I nibble on her ear, kiss the side of her neck. "Say it," I coax, murmuring against the shell of her ear.

"Please fuck me in the ass, Asher."

I shouldn't take it as such a victory, but my wolf pumps the air with his fist. He's doing a backflip in the end zone. Like he thinks I just won Lotta's heart, not just her consent for more pleasure.

I kneel behind her, pushing her legs wide with a nudge from my knees. I pull her ass cheeks apart and line the head of my cock up with her back hole. I apply slow but steady pressure, waiting until she opens for me before I breach her entrance. I grip Lotta's hair in the back and pull up. "Who does this beautiful ass belong to?" I ask in a growl.

"You," she pants.

I work the head of my cock into her, then reach around the front of her hips to stroke her clit as I press in, a centimeter at a time. I sense the moment she relaxes from bracing against the intrusion into pleasure. All the muscles in her back, ass, and pelvic floor give way to allow me in. Her pussy gushes arousal.

I sink two fingers inside her as I slowly pump my cock in and out of her ass.

"Oh Fate...Fate, Fate, Fate," she croons.

"That's right, beautiful. You're taking my big wolf cock in your ass right now, aren't you? Do you like that?"

"Yes." It comes as a gasp. Her fingers fist the comforter.

I try not to slam in too hard as my excitement grows. I have to temper my need to dominate with the equal urge to care for my mate.

This isn't punishment. I've hate-fucked her before, but I realize now that was hurting her. I may have wanted her pain–or thought I wanted it–but now that I've won her tears, I want to punch my own face in.

"Good girl," I praise. "You're taking me like a good girl, aren't you, sweetheart?"

She opens even more for me. I add a third finger to her pussy, as my heart rate skyrockets.

"I'm gonna come in your ass, and then you're going to sit on my lap while I feed you. Got it?" I say it like it's punishment. It's just pure dominance–letting her know she's mine to fuck. Mine to claim. Mine to care for.

She lets out a cry, and I can't wait any longer. I piston

into her tight ass, my balls drawing up tight before I bury deep and release.

"Oh...oh!" she cries.

I groan, shuddering as the pump-action from my balls continues, and I spill even more cum into her.

Once I'm sure I won't accidentally lose control and mark her, I lower my face to kiss her shoulder and neck and the side of her face. She twists her face, and I catch her lips in a passionate kiss.

"Good girl."

* * *

Lotta

Good Girl.

Tonight's the first time Asher's used those words with me.

They should sound wrong coming from my student–*my student!*--but instead, they flood me with warmth.

Now that he's softened, I see how much his anger affected me. It's unnerving how much I crave approval from him. Before tonight I would've sworn up and down that I didn't need it from him or anyone in this town, but it would've been a lie.

What I want from Asher is more than forgiveness or even sex.

I'm looking for something deeper. I'm looking for that spiritual connection. That sense that someone else sees and accepts me for who I am, not just who they want me to be.

I've had far too little of that in my life.

And this big, brutish man is starting to make me believe he does see me. He doesn't accept me yet, but there's knowledge. He pays attention. He responds to my moods. My needs.

And I shouldn't want his acceptance, but dammit, I do.

I want his love. His approval. I want closure from the rift of our past. I want healing and wholeness with him.

Fuck.

I want everything.

And that is so wrong.

I can't have everything. I learned that the hard way when I decided to eschew pack and become an artist.

I go limp as Asher eases out of me. He's wrung so much pleasure out of me, I don't know if I'd remember my ABC's right now. He strokes his large palm down my spine, landing with a rough grip of my ass and then a gentle slap.

I'm in too much bliss to move. My asshole is sore, but my limbs are loose and heavy, and I feel like I'm floating on a cloud.

It's crazy how much I trust my body to a guy who hates me.

But he doesn't completely hate me, does he?

"Up, baby." Asher scoops my limp body into a roll, so I'm face up in his arms. He settles me on one thigh, my legs draped across his lap, so I can lean back against the circle of his arm.

It's heaven.

I love being cradled and protected by his strength. Love being skin-to-skin with him in a post-sex languor. I love having his scent coating my body, so I can't tell where his ends and mine begins.

I tuck my face against his neck and sigh. His dick twitches against my ass, reminding me where he just was. How dirty and dominant this now-gentle giant can be.

He tugs a tote bag closer to us and pulls out a loaf of

what must be fresh-baked bread from Wolf Ridge Sweet Treats.

My stomach rumbles.

He hands it to me. "Here, open this and tear some off. There's meat and cheese to go with it." He pulls out an assortment of charcuterie items, including fresh organic raspberries, olives, artichokes and gourmet cheeses. Then he pours us each a glass of wine.

I don't mean to—it must be the post-sex letdown, but I find tears starting in the corners of both eyes and a wobble in my chin.

Why would I cry?

I hide my face in Asher's neck again, holding my breath to suppress the urge.

Asher strokes my hair, then cradles the back of my head. He must notice that I'm not breathing because he tugs my face away to look at me.

Before I can stop it, I lose a few tears down my cheeks.

"Oh, baby." There's tenderness in his voice. He nestles my head back onto his shoulder and massages the back of my neck.

I'm so grateful he doesn't ask what's wrong.

I'm too proud to tell him that it's about him. That him showing me this level of kindness and attention brought me to tears.

He leans his head against mine. "Let's start over," he murmurs. "Can we do that? Just forget about everything that was our past?"

"Yes." I sniff. "I'd like that." I curl even more into him, craving the comfort he provides.

He responds by tightening his arm around me.

"Forget everything but this moment. Who we are here, together, in our meadow."

I nod against his shoulder, then review his words. "Our meadow?"

"Yeah. This is it, right? From your painting?"

I lift my head, my tears drying with the distraction. "What?"

Asher sweeps an open palm in front of us, like he's presenting the majestic landscape. "This valley?"

I stare at the rock formations and the meadow in front of me, and flashes of purples, blues, and grays swirling on my brush take shape in my mind's eye. The boulders and mountains snap into a familiar shape. I picture the meadow grasses dotted with gold Mexican poppies and draw in a sharp breath.

He's right! This is the landscape in the small painting of us that he stole from me. I twist my neck to look around. Oh wow. This exact landscape is in at least half of my paintings. All the ones that feature the two wolves, black and white. Yin and yang.

My pulse races. Goosebumps prick my arms and the back of my neck.

"Asher"--I sound breathless-- "I've never been here before."

He meets my gaze, his brows popped high. "Never?"

I shake my head.

"You haven't been here before tonight?" he repeats, like he can't believe it.

A sob catches in my belly. The next one surges up my throat, but I don't know why. It has something to do with the magnitude of me painting the two of us in a place where we'd have our first real date long before I knew anything. Before I knew Asher was my mate. Or even that I was painting myself and my fated mate and not two symbolic wolves from my imagination who didn't exist.

Asher's arms tighten around me even more. "You've been painting your future," he murmurs against my hair. "*Our* future."

The sob finds its way out in a silent, wracking breath. "That's...crazy. I mean, I don't see how it's even possible."

I hear a light chuckle from Asher or, rather, feel it in the soft tickle of his breath in my hair. "You don't think your wolf knew our future?"

I cover my mouth with a hand, holding in the tidal wave sized sob that erupts.

"Whoa." Asher rubs a hand up and down my back, rocking me gently like I'm a baby.

I don't even know how to explain the enormity of my emotions, but Asher guesses at them. "The problem is, you think art and wolves don't mix." He's still rocking me. I find it hard to believe that this is the same classroom bully who is ruled by belligerence and rebellion. Right now he seems wise beyond years. "That's because your parents are boneheads."

I let out a watery laugh.

"You locked up your wolf, thinking she wasn't compatible with art. She became your muse. Maybe you thought you'd keep her there, forever. Am I close?"

"Yes." Tears continue to streak my face, and I struggle to take a deep breath. I still don't understand why I'm crying. I just know that Asher verbalizing what I've been living alone with for years is healing me.

"What if...what if she's not separate from you, Lotta? I think you might have it backwards."

I swipe under my eyes with my fingertips.

"What if she's not separate from your art? She could be part of your creative genius, not the foil to it."

I can't believe Asher even knows the word *foil*. This

meat-head jock who refuses to complete any assignments in my class is so much more intelligent and well-educated than he lets on. Every word he speaks is like a truth bomb exploding around me.

"I think we shifters often create separation between our two parts. We say things like, *my wolf got violent. My wolf won't let me back down.* Or *my wolf wants this, but I want that.*" He meets my gaze, and I see distance there–his wounding. "You and I, we try to separate our wolves' attraction from our hatred for each other–"

"I don't hate you, Asher," I blurt, needing to interrupt. "Do you think that?"

Pain flashes in his gaze.

He doesn't understand why I hurt him so deeply before I left. I don't want him to know the real reason my mom had his dad thrown out. She had those council proceedings locked up to protect me and my identity, but I wanted them locked to protect Asher. The truth would crush him–even more now that he knows I'm his mate.

He works to swallow. "*We're starting over.*" Some of the hardness is back in his voice, and it hits me like a blast of cold.

My reaction must show because regret flashes in his hazel eyes. He leans his forehead against mine and whispers it again. "We're starting over, Lotta. This is our beginning, right here, right now."

I nod, rolling my forehead along his. "This is our beginning."

Asher catches my head against his shoulder and kisses the top of it. "Anyway, I think the belief that we are two separate entities in one body instead of one entity in two kind of fucks us."

"But we are ruled by separate urges."

"Yes. But think what we can do when those urges get aligned. If we could get them on the same page."

Resistance drives up in my chest. That opposition I used to push against my parents' desire for me. It's a strength I've depended on to survive without family and pack. If I get confused now, I fear I'll lose that power.

I'll settle in Wolf Ridge in the life my parents wanted for me. Be a high school art teacher and raise pups in the same small town I grew up in. That's not what I want.

"I'm not against you, Lotta," Asher says simply, as if he sensed my defensiveness rising. "I'm for you. Team Carlotta, all the way."

My lips quirk into a grudging smile.

"Whatever that means," he says. He sets the carton of raspberries on my legs and pries it open, then pops one in my mouth.

The flavor bursts on my tongue, seemingly magnified by one thousand. Something about this moment of sensation amplifying my senses. I soak it in–being held on Asher's lap, the words, *Team Carlotta, all the way* echoing in my ears, the last gorgeous purples from the lingering sunset, the endorphins from my orgasms still making me float.

This isn't going to work, a voice in my head insists.

I know she's right, but I don't care. I deserve this moment. This restart with Asher.

This moment, right now.

Another voice whispers something completely audacious. Something I don't even care about. She whispers,

I deserve love.

Chapter Seventeen

*L*otta
    Wednesday after school, I meet Olive at 603, an upscale bar down in Cave Hills. Wolf Ridge has nothing upscale. I can't afford the fifteen dollar drinks here, but it's better than hitting a local bar and being surrounded by pack members who are all up in your business.

I also need the liquid courage, not that the buzz will last the way it does for humans.

"Are you ready for this?" Olive asks, sliding into the seat next to mine.

"Not even remotely." I give her a weak smile. "Thank you so much for doing this with me."

"Of course! Your art is amazing. You deserve to be in the best galleries in the country."

I laugh. "You haven't even seen what I'm painting these days."

"Well, I remember from high school! You've always been an amazing artist."

I'm not sure I can trust her opinion since she's basing

it on my very undeveloped raw talent before I went to college, but it's nice to have someone in my corner. This is the kind of blind support I always craved from my parents.

The kind my spoiled roommate Andy had—the entitled ass who seems to want to hook up with me when he comes to Arizona but ghosted me about the introduction to the gallery he's visiting.

That's part of what made me follow up with Olive about her offer to help. I need to get out there and market myself. I *can't* get stuck in Wolf Ridge teaching art for the rest of my life.

An unexpected shifting in my chest accompanies that thought, though.

I may want to escape Wolf Ridge, but what about Asher?

Up until this week, until our picnic date, I had refused to even consider continuing anything with Asher beyond this teaching stint.

But honestly–I knew that was delusional. I can barely make it through twenty-four hours without having sex with him. Do I really think I'm going to roll out of town at the end of the school year?

Beyond biology, I'm catching feelings. Not that I didn't always have feelings for Asher. I cared deeply about him back when I was tutoring him, before I even knew he was my mate. But now...I'm addicted to his presence. I want more time with him than he gives me. I want conversation and laughter and communion. I want all of Asher. Not just the physical piece he's willing to give me.

Most of all, I want his forgiveness. But how can I get it when I don't want him to know what really happened, and he doesn't want to hear my explanation anyway?

Olive orders a shot of tequila and downs it quickly. "Let's do this." She grins at me.

"Cheers." I swig the rest of my espresso martini and pay for both of our drinks then slide off the barstool and head to my car.

I brought three of the medium-sized canvases along with me because I don't feel like photos accurately represent what I do. I brought an abstract wolf painting that I created in college, a super realistic painting of my white wolf standing in the meadow Asher brought me to, and a whimsical pop-art style wolf painted in bright orange, pink and blue.

Olive carries one, and we enter the first gallery and ask to speak to a manager.

"No unsolicited art," a blonde woman in a boxy suit snaps from where she was hovering mid-gallery.

I freeze.

Olive lifts her chin. "What is your preferred method of contact for artists?"

"Nothing unsolicited," the woman repeats firmly.

Some customers turn and look down their noses at us.

Ugh. This is awful. I'm already walking out the door, my face burning.

Olive mutters, "Don't let that bitch get to you."

"Maybe this wasn't the right way to do it," I say, already defeated. "My roommate from college has a contact at one of the galleries here. I will ask him again if he can introduce me."

"Well, let's just see if someone will be nice enough to tell us how it works." Olive marches on to the next gallery, a few doors down.

This guy practically barricades us from entering. He jumps in front of me as I walk through the door. "You can't bring that in here." He looks alarmed, like my paintings carry an infectious disease that will spread to the art in his gallery.

"Can you help us out? We're just trying to figure out the proper protocol for reaching out to the owner." I have to give Olive credit for not tucking tail at his tone.

The guy's upper lip curls in a sneer. "I'm the owner. Everything here is highly *curated*. We're booked eighteen months in advance with art from all over the world. We're not currently accepting submissions.

"Got it," I mumble, backing out the way I entered and jostling Olive as I do.

"Here's the thing." Olive snatches the two paintings from my sagging arms, stacking them on top of each other. "You can't sell art for exorbitant prices unless you're snobby, so they're all going to be assholes."

I sigh and start back toward the car. This clearly wasn't the right way to make connections.

"We just need to figure out a way to make them think you're the next big thing. Have someone who impresses them give them a call or something. Would one of your professors?"

I deflate even more. "I don't know. My program was full of amazing artists. There's nothing to make me special over any of them. I never had a champion or anything."

"There must be a way."

"Olive, thank you." I wrap my arms around her neck in a hug she can't reciprocate since she's holding all three paintings. "I'm grateful for your confidence in me, but I think I need to go home and regroup. I'll try my college roommate to see if he can make the introduction I need to get into one of these places."

Olive shrugs. "Okay. Fair enough."

We reach the car, and I open the trunk for Olive to put the paintings away.

"Come on," Olive says. "This round is on me, girl."

* * *

Asher

I hate schoolwork. I shouldn't have left this essay until the last minute, but time is always tight with school, football practice, and working weekends at the bakery. Now that I'm ducking out for at least an hour a night to see Lotta, it feels like I'll never catch up on my schoolwork.

It's 8:30 pm, and I'm sitting in front of the school-issued laptop at our kitchen table, staring at a blinking cursor. I have this paper on the *Odyssey* due tomorrow, and I'm barely past the second paragraph. I've spent the week working on the self-portrait Lotta assigned. I guess that's on me–I could be using classtime, like everyone else, but instead I'm still pretending to hate her, fucking around with my friends all hour, and patently refusing to do any work under her watch.

But the truth is, at some point after I stole that little painting of us, I started caring about the idea of making art.

Art that represents us.

Art that tells a story or conveys a meaning. Art that will show Lotta how much she destroyed me. Maybe also give her a glimpse of what she meant to me–means to me.

I've been cutting out tiny pictures from magazines and collecting small mementos, like the logo torn from a Wolf Ridge Sweet Treats bag, and the corner of the first math test I got an A on after she started tutoring me.

Now that I know she's my mate, I don't feel as

demented for saving this shit. For keeping that pendant of hers in my dresser all these years.

My phone buzzes with a text, and I glance down, expecting it to be Abe or Seb or Markley.

It's Lotta.

> Please say you're coming soon.

My lips quirk, and my dick gets chubby. It's the first time Lotta's texted me. For some reason, it feels like a small victory. There's a level of comfort we crossed after the picnic.

> Feeling needy?

I text back.

> Yeah. Need to drown my sorrows with something better than a cocktail.

> This cock is definitely better.

I pause, digesting what she said.

> What sorrows?

> Meh. Olive and I visited a couple of galleries in Scottsdale but they wouldn't even look at my art. It's fine.

It's not fine. I want to slay dragons for her now, but I don't imagine me charging down to art galleries in Scottsdale is going to do much good.

I was trying to finish an essay but fuck it. I'll
be right there.

I slap the laptop shut. My mom looks over from the counter where she's meal-prepping for the next few days. "Are you finished, hon?"

"Uh, not quite. But I'm taking a break."

"Do you have a girlfriend, Asher?" my mom asks.

Crap. I guess I haven't been too slick about hiding where I've been going.

I'm not one to lie to my mom. Shifters can smell lies, so she would know, and it would only be hurtful.

"Yeah. Sort of."

"Does *sort of* mean you're slipping out to see her every night?"

I let out a chagrined chuff. "Yeah."

My mom folds her arms over her chest. "I thought so." She seems pleased. There's a twinkle in her eye. It definitely wouldn't be there if she knew who I was sneaking out to see.

"Well, I'm sure I don't need to have a discussion with you about protection, do I?"

"Definitely not," I say quickly. "We're good."

"So, when do I get to meet this girl?

Never.

The only thing worse than my mom finding out I'm dating Carlotta James would be *her* mom finding out. Both of them would be horrified, I'm sure.

I never told my mom that I was the one responsible for my dad's banishment–that I had told Carlotta about him stealing from the brewery. It was in a moment of anger. My dad had kicked me around before she arrived at our place, and then he embarrassed me in front of her, mocking me for needing a tutor. He called me slow, as I recall.

Carlotta defended me, correcting him. She told him I was perfectly bright, and my grades had improved greatly over the past few months.

Realizing my dad was going to be a dick to her for correcting him, I tugged her out the door, pretending that we needed a book from the library for that night's homework.

She bought me a hamburger at the New Moon diner. I was grumpy, wanting to act out. So I threw my dad under the bus and told her about him stealing from the pack by pocketing money from parking lot fees at the brewery.

"Asher?" my mom prompts when I hesitate.

My mom and I never talked about it, but she knows Carlotta's mom is on the council. She probably put it together who ratted my dad out.

"I don't know, Mom. I'm not sure it's gonna work out with this girl."

My mom's forehead wrinkles. "You're spending every night with this girl," mom points out. "It seems serious to me. Do her parents know?"

Do her parents know that she's screwing one of her students? Uh, that would be a big no.

"No. Not yet. Like I say, mom, I don't know if it's gonna work out. It's all kind of new."

My mom throws me a skeptical look but doesn't say anything else.

My phone buzzes with another text from Lotta.

> Bring your homework, and I will help you with it.

Damn. That offer should not be so hot to me, but it

rekindles that prepubescent obsession I had with her when she was my tutor. Something in my body responds as if I'm still thirteen.

I unplug the laptop and tuck it under my arm before I head out the back door. Outside, I pause, realizing my mom might be brainstorming all the houses within walking distance to our place with she-wolves my age.

Oh well. Considering she just made it clear she's been tracking my behavior, she probably already noted that I'm leaving by the back door on foot every night.

I drop into the shadows and follow the wash up to Lotta's casita. I find the door open. Inside, Lotta's lit candles and has two glasses of lemon water sitting at the breakfast bar that serves as her table.

Something weird happens to my heart–a double thud, or a bounce. Something unnerving.

"Wow. Hey." I clear my throat because it's suddenly constricted. I walk over to where she's sitting and cradle her face, bending down to kiss her softly.

Her lips move against mine.

I'm not sure what happens for her, but I'm suddenly awake. *Alive.* Back on this planet. I'm not sure where I've been until now, but it wasn't here. I wasn't this present. I wasn't standing looking at the most beautiful she-wolf on the planet, drinking in her scent, reveling in the fact that she was waiting for me, with candles lit and drinks poured, ready to help me with the most mundane but necessary work.

And that...feels like *love.*

Which nearly drops me to the floor.

To think that Lotta might care for me makes my heart thud like I'm in the middle of a football game.

When I break the kiss, her gaze is soft. She pulls out the

bar stool beside her and pats it. "Let's get that paper done. What's the assignment?"

I slide into the seat beside her. It feels both as natural as breathing and like an out-of-body experience at the same time. Like I've always belonged beside this beautiful female. Like things have always been this easy between us. Like our destiny is assured.

I pluck her from her seat and lift her onto my lap. Her laugh is low and husky as I pull her hair to the side to kiss the side of her neck.

"Homework first." She attempts to use her teacher voice on me.

My dick lengthens against her soft ass. I find her classroom authority so fucking hot right now. In fact, now that I'm over hating her, I can admit what a brilliant teacher she is. Her enthusiasm for her subject shines through every lecture. Every assignment. She loves art, and she wants her students to love it as deeply and madly as she does.

The weird thing is that it's working. Art never meant anything to me before, but now I see the beauty of it. It evokes something in me. Especially now that I've witnessed the magic of Lotta's muse.

How she foretold our future through her art.

I slide my hand up the inside of her thigh.

She opens my laptop. "You heard me, baller." She slides off my lap to stand between my legs and turns around to face me. Her arms slip behind my neck. "But if you're a good student, there will be a reward." Her voice is sex-kitten sultry, and she flicks her tongue against my earlobe.

I palm her ass and let out a low growl. I'm not sure I can make it through homework without fucking her, but for some reason I want to try. I've been the polar opposite of a good student since the day she showed up at Wolf Ridge

High. I was punishing her for showing her face in my school.

Now it feels wrong.

Reluctantly, I release my grip on her soft curves and turn her back around to face the laptop.

"It's an essay on the Odyssey. I'm supposed to write the story from the perspective of another character."

"Okay, who did you choose?"

"The cyclops."

Lotta's soft laugh wraps around me like a blanket, snuffing any last embers of anger I had toward her.

I stare at her lovely profile as she reads the couple of paragraphs I wrote, and I realize this is it.

I am hopelessly lost for this female.

What happened with my dad will somehow have to coexist with the fact that Lotta is my mate.

I love her. Always have, always will.

Chapter Eighteen

otta

L I wake in a state of deep pleasure. Asher's scent curls all around me. I'm snuggled in the covers of my giant bed, still warm from our love-making last night.

Asher wrote a brilliant, thoughtful essay, surprising me not only with his understanding and knowledge of *The Odyssey* but also with his own creativity and story-telling ability. I rewarded him with a blowjob that turned his eyes bright green and made him tear one of my feather pillows in half, filling the casita with feathers.

I reach for my phone to see how much time I have before my alarm goes off and find I can't move. Strong, warm arms engulf me.

Asher. My mate.

He stirs behind me, arms tightening with my movement. "Oh damn, I spent the night," he murmurs against my skin. "Sorry, I'll sneak out in a minute." He nudges me onto my belly. "Right after I get inside your perfect pussy."

I spread my legs wide for him, sighing contentedly into the bedsheets.

Obviously, this is risky. The chance of one of my parents or a neighbor seeing him leave my place is so much higher when it's light out, but I can't find it in me to care.

It feels too good to have Asher's rapidly hardening cock sliding between my legs, pressing against my entrance. I lift my ass, and he enters me, stroking inside with slow, languid movements.

I hum a low incantation of enjoyment.

Asher rolls us to our sides and continues the long, slow strokes. Then he brings his fingertip to my clit. I'm too relaxed from sleep to come, but it feels glorious when he traces a light circle there. Asher doesn't seem to be in any hurry to come, either. He holds my hip to thrust up into me as he nibbles on my neck.

"Yum," I murmur.

"Mmm." There's a wolfy growl to his voice. He picks up the intensity of his thrusts, fingers tightening on my hip.

"Get up here." He rolls to his back, so I'm straddling his hips. "Work for me, sweetheart." He grips my ass and urges me over his dick. My hands fall to his shoulders. I'm dripping wet, grinding my clit down on him as I slide forward and back.

"More," he commands.

The slackness of my muscles vanishes. Tension coils in my low belly, and my breath quickens.

Asher's eyes glow green.

"I see your wolf," I pant.

"I see yours." He holds my hips still and thrusts up into me a dozen times then pulls me forward and back over him again. I'm getting close.

"Give it to me." He reaches up and pinches one of my

nipples, rolling and tugging it, making me squeeze around his dick with the answer tug below my waist. "Give it all to me."

I don't know if he means my orgasm or my life.

At this moment, I'm inclined to give him both, which should terrify me but instead makes me feel like I'm sailing on the downslope of a rollercoaster.

I bounce over his cock, head thrown back, then brace one hand against the headboard and go to town, riding as fast as I can.

"That's it." When I break the rhythm, he rolls us on the big bed, so I'm on my back, and he's above me and drives into me. "Now you're going to feel me."

I laugh through my pants. "Like I wasn't feeling you before?"

He flicks his brows and thrusts in hard, holding the side of my neck to keep my head from driving into the headboard.

"Yes!" I gasp.

Asher gives it to me hard but, somehow, also loving. Attentive. So different from the rough, cold sex we began this relationship with. He's killing me with kindness now, and it's more than I can take.

I clutch at his shoulders, hook my ankles behind his back to urge him in with my legs. We work frantically together, like this climax will determine if we win or lose. Live or die.

And I'm living for Asher now.

Dying for him, too.

And I don't even know yet what I've won and what I've lost. All I know is that I'm here for it. For all of it. Whatever this journey with Asher may bring.

"Come for me. Are you going to come for me like a good

girl?" Asher's words are rough and guttural. He's about to lose control.

"Yes!" At the suggestion, my ass lifts and my internal muscles start to squeeze, wringing out pulses of pleasure.

Asher groans and thrusts in deep. I swear I feel the hot ribbons of his essence filling me as I orgasm. For the first time, I have that proprietary sense of wanting to keep the evidence of him being inside me. Wanting others to know this magnificent male wolf belongs to me now.

But of course, I can't claim him. Not if I want to keep my job.

I feel the scrape of his tooth against my neck, and I shove him away before he sinks into my flesh. "Asher!" I pant. "You can't." I meet his green gaze and try to show him with mine that I understand. That I feel it, too. I want it, too. "My job," I say.

He nods jerkily and pulls out, rolling me to my belly and slapping my ass. "I know, Teacher," he says lightly. "But that doesn't change the fact that you're mine."

* * *

Asher

After practice that afternoon, I walk Abe to his Range Rover, glancing over my shoulder toward the art studio as we walk. Lotta's still in there, painting. She stays late every evening, long past when we leave football practice.

Since the picnic in the meadow, Lotta's been softer. Sex is less frenetic. I stay around for a little while after or bring food over before. They aren't long, intense dates, but there's more ease between us. The brittleness is gone from our interactions.

When I'm away from her, I find myself craving more

than her body. I crave conversation. Closeness. I want to consume all of Lotta James—not just her body but her mind, her soul.

But that would take trust. And trust is one thing we don't have. I told Lotta we could restart. That means I have to block out the past from my mind. Forget that mile-deep wound she inflicted in my life.

And I've been thinking about what would make her trust me. I was thinking about how she was down last night about visiting galleries without any luck.

I've been a dick to her, I know. But it also occurred to me that Lotta doesn't really trust anyone, and I suspect it has a lot to do with the way her parents fucked her up about her art.

They never should have made her choose between pack and career. And I shouldn't say *career,* because art is more than a career to Lotta. It's her soul. Her identity.

And that's why I have to lean in there.

"What's up?" Abe says when we're out of earshot of anyone else.

"I wondered if I could talk to your mate about something."

In a flash, Abe has me pinned against his vehicle, his eyes glowing with his wolf.

I laugh, holding up my hands. "Relax. It's about Lotta. You can be there for protection if you want."

Abe blinks, his wolf receding. He releases me and gives his head a shake to snap his neck. "Sorry, man. Just instinct."

"Yeah. No worries. I get it."

"So... yeah. Do you want to go over there now?"

I nod. "Did you tell her about me and Lotta?"

Abe frowns. "No, dude. You swore me to secrecy."

"Right, yeah. Thanks. I mean, we could tell her if you think she can keep a secret. Or I can just not use specifics."

"She can keep a secret." He sounds offended on her behalf. "Her twin doesn't even know they're bears."

"Okay, cool. I'll follow you over to her place?"

"Yeah. See you there."

I climb on my bike and trail Abe to the mansion on Moongaze Hill where Lauren and Lincoln Sterling live. The twins moved here this school year from Manhattan, and their human and wealth status inspired instant hatred in all of Wolf Ridge. Now that Abe marked Lauren as his mate, though, they're under his protection, and things have changed for them socially.

I follow Abe up to the hand-carved door. Inside, the sound of a piano stops playing, and Lauren comes to the door. Her soft gaze lands on Abe then skips to me, and she raises a quizzical brow.

"Hey, Lauren. I, uh, wondered if I could pick your brain about New York. And art stuff."

Her brows pop, but she holds the door open wide. "Of course. Come on in."

"Thanks." I have no idea if this is a hare-brained idea or not, but I figure it's worth a shot.

As we enter the house, the sounds of killer electric guitar playing come from the hallway. I jerk my thumb in that direction. "Is that your brother playing?"

Lauren sits on the couch, and Abe slides in right beside her, an arm draped behind her back. "Yeah. He's pretty good."

"And you were playing the piano?" I take a seat in the chair opposite them.

"Did you come here to flirt with my girl or ask art questions?" Abe cuts in, and I grin at his possessiveness. I hold my palms out. "Art questions. Chill, bro."

Lauren rolls her eyes, but I can tell she loves it.

"So...this is probably a wild goose chase, but you're sophisticated, and you came from New York. I wondered if you know anything about the New York art scene? Like how to get into galleries?" As I say the words, I realize how ridiculous I sound. "Nevermind, this was a dumb idea." I stand.

"It's not dumb."

I sink back into the chair.

"We know some fairly big-time artists. Like the kind who sell paintings for fifty thousand dollars."

"Whoa. Okay. So any advice?"

"I mean...are you thinking about art school?"

I let out a harsh laugh. "It's not for me. She already graduated from the most prestigious art school in the country."

"Ohhhh–*she*." Lauren looks at me speculatively. "Ms. James." She glances at Abe for confirmation.

"Would it be okay if we kept this between us?" I ask. "Abe knows, but that's it."

Lauren's lips curve. "Scandalous."

"Please, Lauren. It's not my life that would be ruined if it got out."

Lauren mimes locking her lips with a key. "My lips are sealed." She throws the imaginary key over her shoulder. "So, yeah. There are gallery owners you can approach. I can ask my dad if he can connect me with one of our family friends to get some specific contacts if you want."

"Really?" This went way better than expected. "Yeah. I mean, yes, please. I would really appreciate that, Lauren."

"No problem. I'll talk to my dad tonight at dinner and get back to you. Want me to text you?"

"No way you're getting my girl's phone number," Abe interrupts.

Lauren rolls her eyes again. "We'll group chat then."

* * *

Lotta

The next night Asher meets me at school as I'm cleaning up to come home. "Am I late again?" I ask breathlessly when I open the locked door for him.

He picks me up to straddle his waist, the same way he did last time.

I wriggle. "The janitor's still here," I whisper, and he drops me immediately, sending me a boyish, dimpled grin that makes my insides melt.

"You're not late, I just wanted to take some measurements." He pulls a measuring tape from his jeans pocket as he strides down the hallway to my studio.

"Measurements?"

"Yeah. I'm gonna frame your paintings."

I stop walking. "What?"

He turns and grins. "You heard me, Ms. James." He tilts his head toward the studio. "I watched a Youtube video on how to DIY frames and save hundreds of dollars."

I'm still melting. Scrape me off the floor where I've become a puddle.

I jog to catch up with him, looking around quickly for the janitor before I loop my arm through his. "Thank you. That would be amazing. My paintings do need frames. I mean, I don't think that would've helped at the galleries–it was more a gatekeeping thing, but..."

We're inside the studio now, and Asher stops my words with a kiss.

I melt against him, my arms looping up around his neck, my body softening into his. "That was really thoughtful, Asher. Thank you."

He kisses me again, but he's a man with a mission. He strides back to the stack of paintings and starts to measure and inventory them. "These have names?" he asks, ripping a piece of paper from my sketchbook and thrusting it at me. "Will you write down the name of each one and a description, so I know which is which then I'll put the dimensions underneath."

It takes over an hour, but Asher doesn't seem to mind. By the end of it, I have a list of every painting I've made over the last five years. The paintings I had to go into debt on my credit card to ship back here.

"Wow. I've produced a lot of art." I look at the list. It feels satisfying. Not that I'm a quantity-over-quality kind of artist, but it's nice to see what a long list of art I have available to sell, if I can ever get in a gallery.

"Have you thought about an Etsy store?" Asher asks.

My brows pop. I notice the same resistance rise up in me that I had when Olive suggested we visit galleries. Is it fear of putting myself out there? Or my wolf instinct telling me it's a bad move?

It's not like the gallery visits went well for me.

"Well, no…"

Asher shrugs. "I'm just thinking it might be another way to get your stuff out there. I mean, in addition to galleries and what-not."

"Um, yeah. I mean, I don't have the slightest idea how to go about that, but I should figure it out."

"Yeah. Or I'll figure it out, and you keep painting."

Asher folds the two-page list of paintings into squares and tucks it in his back pocket. "Also, I have a surprise for you."

"You do?"

"Yep. It's at Sweet Treats."

"Aren't they closed?"

"I have keys. Meet me in the back alley in fifteen minutes." Asher ushers me out the door of the studio into the hall.

"I'll beat you there," I tease him.

"No chance of that, swee–Ms. James." He winks at me, looking over his shoulder to see if anyone's still around. "See you soon," he mouths before jogging a few steps ahead and slipping out the door in front of me.

I pretend not to watch him start up his motorcycle as I walk to my car, but the entire time there's a low happy buzz in my chest.

I'm loving this new level of comfort with Asher. It seems he's finally forgiven me for getting his dad banished. I still don't know how things are going to work for us–especially when he's my student for the rest of the school year, and I want to leave Arizona when it's over–but it's starting to feel like the insurmountable problems are worth solving.

Maybe I'd be willing to stay. I don't know.

My phone buzzes, and I glance down, thinking it might be from Asher.

It's from Andy, though.

Andy:

> I'm in Phoenix. Come swim at the resort–
> they have a lazy river.

My stomach twists. Even texting feels like an infidelity to Asher.

Me:

Not interested.

Andy:

Meeting at the gallery is tomorrow evening.
You can tag along to my meeting.

I suck in a breath. My wolf says this is a bad idea. Artist me says sacrifices have to be made. Not with Andy–fuck that, never that–but I need to use the connections I have. I'm not afraid of saying no to Andy–even if he does seem to be acting illogically attached to me. I'm a shifter. No human man could ever force his will on me. Asher would hate me meeting with him, especially if he knew how much Andy has been up my skirt, but I'll keep it short and business-like. End of story.

Me:

Send me the name and address.

Andy:

I'll pick you up.

Me:

It's not even remotely on the way.

Andy:

Come with me or don't, babe.

Ugh. Really? What a pain in my ass. He's purposely jerking my chain.

Me:

> Fine. Pick me up at the school so I can put
> a few of my paintings in the car.

Andy:

> Send the address.

I send the address and start the car, trying to ignore the queasiness in my belly. I should tell Asher.

I will tell him. But not until right before Andy comes. I don't want his wolf to get crazy possessive and for him to act irrationally.

I shove down my misgivings as I turn the ignition and drive to the alley behind Sweet Treats. Once I'm there, I forget the whole thing because Asher's leaning against the old brick building that used to be a mill. It belongs to Mrs. Angelson, who owns the bakery, but I don't think she uses it for anything.

I climb out of the car.

Asher looks up and down the alleyway then beckons me to the door. He turns the knob when I get there and ushers me in.

I've looked in the windows in the past. It looked like old equipment and storage bins. I suck in a breath when I take in the scene now.

The place has been completely cleaned up. Storage bins are stacked neatly at one end, but at the other, drop cloths have been spread, and there's an easel set up in front of the window.

"I thought you could use this as your studio. You know— if you don't want to paint at school." Asher flashes a grin.

His dimples break my heart. Literally split it right in

two. I'm a puddle, warm and glowy and completely done-for. Asher has conquered my every resistance.

When I don't say anything, he says, "Or no big deal if you prefer working at school."

"No," I say quickly, running to throw my arms around his waist. "I freaking love this. Thank you so much. Are you sure it's okay? I mean, with Mrs. Angelson?"

"Totally sure. She's happy to have it used by someone." His hands slide down my back and grab my ass. "And it gives us another safe place to meet until the end of the school year."

"Oh yeah?" I purr, sliding my hands under his shirt to get to bare skin. "Are you going to put a mattress in here?"

"I'll figure something out." His voice is a low growl as he picks me up by the waist and carries me toward the storeroom. "I need to taste that pussy of yours right now."

"Uh uh," I disagree. "I'm tasting you first tonight. Put me down, big guy. I'm going to show you my thanks."

Chapter Nineteen

Asher

For the second night in a row, I sleep at Lotta's. This time it wasn't an accident.

She didn't kick up a fuss yesterday, so I figure it's now allowed. It's way hard to leave her bed when she's naked and warm and coated in my fluids. I set an alarm, so I'm up before dawn.

"Asher..." Lotta rolls over to face me. I brush the black hair back from her smooth skin. She's so fucking beautiful. "What do you want to do after high school?"

"This," I answer immediately. Because this is it for me. I've arrived. Sleeping in Lotta James' bed is more of a future than I ever imagined for myself.

I sense a touch of worry in her, though, so I sober. She wants out of this town, I know that.

"Coach thinks I might get a football scholarship somewhere." I shrug. "It's not like college is a dream for me or anything, but I'm also not tied to Wolf Ridge, if that's what you're asking."

"You should take a scholarship if you can get one. Get out of this town."

"Yeah. Okay." I sure as fuck hope she means with her.

I roll out of bed. "I have something for you." I pick up my backpack and pull out the canvas I used to make my "self-portrait." They're due today in class, but I wanted to give it to her personally.

I hand her the little canvas, and she takes it with shaky fingers. It's a multi-media collage. I covered the canvas with cut out pictures of things that remind me of us. I study her face as she takes in the piece.

She sucks in a sharp breath when she sees the gold moon pendant glued across the center. It hits me like a slap to the face.

The blood drains from her face. "H-how did you get that?" Her voice shakes. "Did your dad give that to you?" she's panting, like she can't catch her breath. "Or... *your mom?*"

"What are you talking about?"

Her gaze is unfocused, like she's searching for a memory. Then she drops the canvas on the floor and scrambles to her feet like we're about to have a fight. "Did you...*did you know?*"

Something is terribly wrong. Lotta's upset, and my wolf would do anything to fix it.

I spread my hands to show her wolf I'm no threat. "Know what?"

Her eyes are wild. There's fear and trauma in her scent. *What the fuck is going on?*

"Have you known this whole time?" She looks at me in horror.

I take a step closer, but she backs away. "Lotta, what are you talking about?"

She searches my face. Blinks. Then exhales. "Oh." She shakes her head, looking to the floor. She stoops to pick up the canvas, but I have a feeling it's just to hide her face from me. I know I'm right when she comes up completely composed.

"I was just confused for a minute. Did I–Where did you, um, find my necklace?"

I stare at the necklace trying to decode what just happened. She freaked out when she saw it.

Asked if my dad gave it to me.

Why would my dad–

I snatch the canvas from her hand and rip the necklace off, pulling up most of the collage with it. I hold it up. "What happened? *What happened with my dad?*"

I try to remember the last time I saw her before my dad was banished. It was the night I'd told her about him stealing. She hadn't shown up the next afternoon for our session. And by the night after, he was banished.

"Nothing. It just reminded me of–of tutoring you. Before he left, that's all."

I stare at her, then look down at the necklace lying across my palm. There's something here I don't understand.

Lotta's beautiful cornflower blue eyes fill with tears. What's in her expression? Regret? Yes, but something else. Something that looks like a wound. Like she's been hurt.

I suddenly feel like I've been knocked to my knees. Or perhaps I do drop to my knees–I'm not sure. The room is spinning. I'm hot. My canines have dropped.

"Did he…" It's hard to speak. My larynx is being dragged along a rusty blade. "Did he hurt you?" I can barely rasp the words out.

She holds her hands up, as if to wave away my anger.

189

"Your mom stopped him," she says quickly. "Nothing happened. He tried, that's all."

Tried.

My vision turns red. Rage explodes all around me. My dad laid hands on my mate. Assaulted her! I'm going to kill the bastard.

And I had it backwards all this time. I thought she'd done him wrong. Oh fate.

I let out a howl of rage.

I'm not sure when I shifted, but my four paws scrabble over Lotta's polished saltillo tile. I'm slamming into walls, knocking over furniture, trying to get out of confinement.

Lotta throws open the door, and I bolt for the outdoors.

I need to hunt my progenitor and kill him.

* * *

Lotta

My vision goes wavy, and I clap a hand over my mouth to hold in a sob. My casita feels like a tiny card house in Asher's wake. There are claw marks on the wall. A broken barstool lies on its side on the floor.

My mate is in so much pain.

In this moment, with the advantage of hindsight, I'm sure I did the right thing. My wolf or my muse or whatever part of me it is that sees into my future was guiding me when I swore the council to secrecy about what happened.

There'd been a mix-up about where I was supposed to meet Asher. I'd told him I couldn't make it to Sweet Treats after school, but I'd come to his house later, but he was waiting at the bakery for me. His dad pulled me into the house. He was angry with me for defending Asher the day before, and he launched into a tirade against me, how I was uppity like my mom, and that pack royalty shouldn't exist.

And then his aggression got physical. I don't know why I couldn't shift to defend myself–probably he had some form of alpha command that held me in place. All I remember is that he had me pinned against a wall with my shirt half-torn when Asher's mom walked in and beat him off. Only then did I shift and run straight home.

I ran into my house coated in the scent of fear and drunken shifter. There was no hiding what had happened from my parents, and my mom wasn't going to allow the man who laid a finger on her daughter to remain in the pack.

It had been a horrific, vicious decision.

I didn't want to hurt Asher. My mom said I'd be protecting him and his mom because his dad was a monster who hurt them both. She said I had the opportunity to rid him from their lives, and the pack would thank me.

I made one stipulation. I asked that the council proceedings be sealed from the pack before I spoke. I was underage, so everyone thought it was about protecting my privacy, but it wasn't. It was for Asher. Even then, not knowing he was my mate, I intuited how much this knowledge would hurt him.

I recounted the attempted assault, and I told them about Asher's dad stealing money from the till at the brewery. I asked that if they ever needed to give a public reason for his banishment, his thieving was why. My mom had spent all night before the meeting digging up proof of his on-going crimes, so it wasn't just my word.

When I returned and realized how much Asher hated me, I'd questioned my decision. Not because I needed his understanding–I was willing to be the villain to him. It was because it seemed he'd suffered terribly anyway. The pack had treated him like shit without even knowing what happened. But now, seeing his anguish at finding out the truth, I'm sure I did the right thing. Feeling wronged by me allowed him to have a sense of righteous anger and rebellion. He retained his dignity. Had he borne the shame of his father's deeds through his teen years, I fear he would've shut down completely. Perhaps even left town, as well.

And then I probably never would've met my fated mate.

My morning alarm goes off, making me start. I swing the door shut and look around.

Crap. What should I do?

Asher's hurting. I want to help. I need to help him. I wish I would've shifted immediately and followed him. Now there's no way I'd catch up to him.

I glance at the clock. Dammit.

I take a quick shower, grab an apple to eat, and drive to Sweet Treats. Asher's mom should be working today.

She and I have avoided each other since the incident. I'm not sure why. I think I was ashamed for leaving her to fight her husband alone that night. She was probably ashamed for what happened. Neither of us have spoken about it—which now strikes me as really fucked up and weird.

I park in front and walk in. Mrs. Angelson gives me a wave from the kitchen door. "Hi there, Carlotta! I heard you were back in town!"

"Hi, Mrs. A!"

I force myself to meet Mrs. Martin's gaze and step close to the counter. "Um, good morning, Mrs. Martin. H-have you seen Asher?"

There's no surprise in her expression, but her brow furrows. "No," she says slowly. "He didn't come home last night." She studies me. "I guess I thought he might be with you."

"He was," I say. "But, um..." I swallow. "This morning he found out about..." My heart thunders against my sternum, and my palms are wet. I haven't spoken about the incident since the council meeting. "It came out this morning." I try and fail to swallow. "--what happened with his dad. And Asher wolfed out and ran." My eyes swim with tears.

Asher's mom goes pale. She comes out from behind the counter. To my shock, she pulls me into an awkward hug. "Thank you." Her voice is taut.

"For...what?"

"For caring about my son."

I fight my tears. "Of course I care. I mean, I'd care anyway, but...he's my *mate*." I whisper the last words.

Mrs. Martin jerks away to stare at me in surprise.

I nod. She throws her arms back around me, this time in a tight embrace. "Oh, that's incredible." I hear happy tears in her voice, as if I'd just told her I'm pregnant or something. But fated matches are rare enough that it is worth crying over. Most wolves never find their one true mate, they just make a life with a shifter who's compatible. "What a blessing–for you both."

"Yes, but that's why finding out what happened drove Asher to madness."

She releases me again, her expression clouded. "Yes. Yes, I see. Well, it needed to come out at some point. Give him some time and space to cool off and process this–it's a lot to work through. You go on to school, and I'll call him in as absent. Hopefully he will run off his anguish and come back before dark."

Before dark.

Fate, that makes my heart ache. I don't want Asher out there alone in anguish. I don't want him in anguish at all.

"Go on," Mrs. Martin urges. "I'll be sure he contacts you when he's back."

"Okay, thank you." I squeeze Mrs. Martin's shoulder.

She gives me a fierce hug. "I'm so happy for you both. Don't fret over this. Fate throws curve-balls. It makes us nimble." Her smile is sad, though, reminding me that Fate has thrown her far more than her share of curveballs.

I owe it to her as much as to myself and Asher to make sure we work our stuff out.

As I climb into my car, a text comes in on my phone. My heart leaps, illogically hopeful it might be from Asher.

It's not. It's from Andy.

Andy:

> See you at 5

Nope. This isn't happening. Asher needs me.

Me:

> Sorry—I can't go. Something came up.
> Good luck, though.

194

Chapter Twenty

sher

A I feel the impact before I hear the crunch of metal crushing. Glass shatters all around me. My body is launched into the air and hurled fifty feet to the side of the highway, where I roll.

The sound of brakes squealing reminds me to get back on my feet and run away from human eyes.

Blood soaks my fur. Some of my bones are broken, but I ignore the pain.

Fuck, where am I?

I become dimly aware of the fact that my paws are scraped and bloody, and I'm far, far out of wolf territory. I'm halfway to the Grand Canyon, deep in bear country. And I will *not* win a fight against a bear shifter if I run across one.

I look up at the sky. By the placement of the sun, I would guess it's past noon.

I've been running for hours, blind to my path. Blind to anything but vengeance.

Except I have absolutely no ability to execute that

vengeance. I don't know where my dad is or even where to start looking for him.

Clearly my brain went off-line when I wolfed out and ran.

Lotta.

Oh, fate. I ran off and left my mate. I should've taken her into my arms and held her. Dropped to my knees and begged her forgiveness for being such an ass. Instead, I raged out and ran.

Hardly honorable mate behavior.

I wheel around. I need to get back to her. I abandoned my mate when I should've been there for her–twice.

Fuck. I need to get back as quickly as I can.

* * *

It takes me an eternity to get home. My brain has kicked in enough for me to realize I shouldn't run straight to school in wolf form. Especially not bloody and limping as I am. I stop at my place and rinse off the blood, dust, and brambles in the shower. Several of my ribs and my lower leg are broken, and the pain of their regrowth is worse than the impact of that car that hit me.

And thank fuck it did because it knocked the sense back into me. If it hadn't, I might be in Colorado by now. I wince as I hurriedly get dressed. School is already over, but Lotta will still be there.

I climb on my motorcycle and drive to school.

The team is out on the field. Coach Jamison puts his hands on his hips when he sees me. When I stalk toward the school, he blows his whistle and throws his hands in the air with a *what the fuck?* gesture.

I ignore him. Already desperate to see Lotta and apologize, now something has the hairs on my arms standing up.

Something feels off. Something besides what happened this morning.

I pull open the door to the school.

"Asher! What are you doing?" Coach yells.

I jog down the hallway to the art studio, the hairs on the back of my neck standing up.

Through the window of the door, I see another figure standing in the art studio with Lotta. A man.

A man is with my mate.

My logical brain tries to stop me. It's probably the principal. Or the janitor. Or another teacher. It could be another student. My illogical thought is that it's my dad.

A haze of red-brown covers my vision.

I know it's not true, but my wolf needs to make sure. I have to eliminate all threats to my mate.

I grip the door handle hard enough to bust the hardware, but manage to stop myself before I yank. I try to force in a calming breath. I shouldn't open this door. Lotta needs our relationship to remain a secret. How bad will it look if I go barging in there, and she's with another teacher?

My wolf doesn't give a fuck. He's in a frenzy. He needs to get between Carlotta's body and that other guy's at all costs.

I squeeze my eyes closed, leashing the intense possessiveness I feel. I can't show that here. I can't show anything. I can't fuck up this job for Lotta.

I grip the door knob and turn it slowly, silently. Lotta and her visitor are now hidden from my vantage point, standing behind the canvases in her makeshift studio.

"No, but the question is, what are you going to do for

me?" There's a sexually suggestive lilt to the man's voice that makes me nearly shift. I want to tear him apart with my teeth and watch his blood spill all over the linoleum tile floor.

As I storm across the classroom, I hear the sound of a light slap. "Get off me, Andy." There's no ambiguity to her tone.

That's all the green light I need to kill this guy. I somehow manage not to fling aside every canvas that stands in the way of me seeing them. I make it around the corner only knocking one easel over.

There, I find some asshole human crowding Lotta's space, his hands resting on both her hips, his smiling face leaning close to her frowning one.

"*She said get off.*" There's an inhuman growl to my voice.

"*Asher!*"

The alarm on Lotta's face doesn't register soon enough for me to check my aggression. I don't know what she was going to say, but it's too late. Nothing can stop me now.

I pick up Lotta's visitor by the throat, draw my arm back and hurl him forward through the air. My healing ribs crack, rebreaking from the effort.

I forgot he was human. I forgot to hold back my strength.

He smashes through the plate glass window, his body continuing to soar through the air another twenty feet where he lands in a roll on the grass outside.

"Asher, no!" Lotta shrieks, her eyes wide with horror.

Her upset should slow me down, but instead my wolf only registers that she's still in danger. I stomp across the broken glass, and kick out the remaining pieces along the frame, so I can jump out and finish him off.

"Asher!" Lotta jumps on my back, her forearm against

my windpipe like she can choke me. I hardly feel her weight. I'm oblivious to what she wants from me.

My focus is on the human climbing to his feet, apparently still capable of walking. He won't be soon.

"Asher, no!" She bites my ear.

I jerk my head away, but she clamps her teeth down harder, breaking the skin. Blood drips down my neck.

Some question pops in my mind about what's happening, but I can't focus.

She puts her hands over my eyes, so I can't see.

I pause, finally registering that she's trying to stop me.

"Asher, *you have to stop now.*"

Reality starts to seep in through the fog of rage. Reality and a whisper of dread.

Oh, fuck. *What have I done?*

My breath is coming in hard. I take a step back and then another.

Lotta uncovers my eyes, and I stare at the mess I've made.

"Fuck."

"It's okay." Lotta sounds like she's trying to talk herself into it, too. "He's still alive. He doesn't even look hurt. You get out of here now. I will handle this."

I stay frozen where I am. The enormity of what I've done hits me like a bowling ball to the stomach. I just attacked a human. I broke the biggest pack rule, right after never revealing our nature to humans. Fuck, I broke that one, too. Because that guy just had a taste of my super human strength.

"Fuck, Lotta. I'm sorry. I–I didn't mean to." I'm still staring at the guy staggering around on the grass. "I mean, I did, but I lost control."

"I *know*. He was assaulting me. You couldn't help it.

But Asher, you can't tell them I'm your mate. Let me handle this. Please?"

Oh.

Oh, fuck.

This is it—the moment I always knew would come. I'm going to be banished like my father was. I became the man I now want to kill.

If I tell them Lotta's my mate, I might be released from culpability. They would understand there's nothing more powerful than a male wolf's need to protect his fated mate. Everyone knows that, whether they have a fated mate or not.

But I won't do that to Lotta. As much as it's killing me, she needs us to remain a secret. She needs this job, and I have to respect her wishes. Especially when she directly asked me not to tell.

It's all right. I was never going to be able to make it on the straight and narrow path, anyway. I would've tried for Lotta, but it's too late now. After the shit I've put her through, the best thing I can do for her is leave.

She didn't want to be cuffed to me, anyway. She made that plain from the beginning. She doesn't want to be a wolf or have a mate.

I take another step backward.

Lotta splits her glances between the man out on the grass and me.

There's blood dripping from my hands. I must've grasped the jagged window frame when I was trying to get out.

"Asher—go," Lotta hisses. "Get out of here. You will only make things worse. I'm going to fix this."

I hold no faith in her ability to fix this. But yeah. I'm resigned to this fate.

I was never going to get the happy ending. I was never going to have a mate who wanted me to claim her. Her parents were never going to accept our mating. This town was never going to support me after what my father did, and now I don't blame them.

"Yeah. Okay. I'm gone."

The weight of two tanks fill my limbs as I turn and jerkily walk away.

Chapter Twenty-One

Lotta

"Oh my God! You must be made of rubber!" I make my voice sound cheery, as if I'm congratulating Andy on getting defenestrated.

He's not the sharpest tool in the shed. And it doesn't look like he's actually hurt. So I just might be able to smooth this over.

I have to–for Asher.

"What the fuck?" Andy staggers to his feet.

"Seriously, did you see that?" I stand in the broken window and make my eyes wide with wonder. "You just flew through a plate glass window without a scratch. That's amazing. If I had that on video, it would go viral."

Andy shakes the glass out of his hair.

In my peripheral vision, I see Coach Jamison intercept Asher and escort him in the direction of the parking lot.

Oh fate. He's probably going to take him straight to the sheriff's. Or to Alpha Green. I want to run after him and stop him, but containing the Andy situation is the most important thing. If I can't lock this up tight, Asher's fate will be sealed, and the pack will be at risk.

But I can still fix this. If there's one thing I learned in the last four years, it's how to play in the world of humans. That's something most people in this town don't understand.

Andy's spoiled. His parents are rich. If he takes offense over this, there will be hell to pay. But he's also an egotistical idiot. So if I can make him feel special instead of affronted, I just might be able to avert the criminal and legal nightmare this could become.

Then we can deal with the pack punishment Asher will face.

I have far less leverage there.

"I don't know if I would say *without a scratch*." Andy dabs a spot of blood on his cheek. He's clearly still stunned and disoriented from the attack.

"No, really. You are the luckiest person alive. A stuntman couldn't have done a more beautiful job. You did a full twist in the air and then tucked and rolled. Hang on– I'm coming out there."

Principal Olsen and three other teachers are already jogging out the doors toward him.

I have to beat them there. I grab a paint rag and spread it over the busted glass in the windowsill, then vault out like I, too, am a stunt double.

It occurs to me that a wolf shifter could make a decent living as a stunt double if they wanted.

"Wow, did you guys see that?" I call out, my face bright with excitement. "My friend, Andy, just went through that window without a scratch. It was epic!"

The principal and teachers are all wolf shifters. They understand the necessity of keeping human-wolf relations at peace. They're quick to follow my lead. I watch as their expressions of urgency and concern blink away. They slow their approach.

"What happened?" Principal Olsen asks, shoving his hands in his pockets for a more casual look.

I join Andy in brushing glass off his clothing. It's everywhere–tiny pieces in every wrinkle of fabric. "Well, one of my students walked in on Andy not taking no for an answer, and he picked him up and somehow–I have no idea how–sent Andy through the window. But it's okay. Andy's fine, thank God."

"Thank God," Mrs. Miller, the Chemistry teacher, echoes.

"You weren't taking no for an answer?" Principal Olsen uses the sternness of Alpha Command in his voice. While Andy won't have the extreme biological response to it that shifters do, he should feel cowed by it.

Andy's face, already ruddy from the altercation, goes an even deeper red. There's nothing like shame when it comes to a spoiled rich artist who cares far too much about being admired by others. "Well, I–"

"It's all right," I interrupt. I have the conversation going exactly the way I want it. I get to be the magnanimous one now, instead of Andy. I'm the offended party, but I prevent Andy from going on the defensive by propping up his ego with my warmth. "I'm just relieved no one was hurt." I meet his gaze and shake my head. "Seriously, you were amazing. And so lucky. You should definitely buy a lottery ticket today."

"Wow, that's crazy," Mrs. Miller echoes. Thank fate she's quick on the uptake. "So lucky. Are you into martial arts?"

Andy preens a little. "No. Just naturally athletic."

Principal Olsen looks at me. "Do you want to press charges?"

Andy's head whips around.

"No, definitely not. It was not a big deal. No harm, no foul, right, Andy?"

He blinks at me then at Principal Olsen.

I hold my breath. Please let this work.

Please, please, please let this work.

"Yeah. All good. I'm sorry." He shakes out his designer t-shirt for any remaining pieces of glass.

"No, me, too." I put my hand on his elbow and escort him toward the parking lot. The sooner I get him out of this town, the better.

Andy shakes his head as we walk. "How did...how did I go through the window?"

"It was just some freak accident. Seriously epic. I wish you could have seen yourself."

"What happened to that kid?" He looks around. "I mean, where's the student who threw me?"

"He was really embarrassed. I sent him back to the office." I roll my eyes. "These meathead ballers don't realize how strong they are. He didn't mean you any harm. I obviously knew I wasn't in any danger from you, but he walked in right at the wrong moment. And these jocks all have this damsel in distress savior complex." I flick an imaginary piece of glass from his shoulder. "You're totally okay, right?"

I can see his pride warring with the spoiled part of him that wants to cry victim. "Yeah," he says finally.

My pulse is a quick beat in both my wrists. "Yeah, me too." I'm still pretending I'm the real victim here. I bump my shoulder against his as we walk. "Not cool demanding sexual favors in return for introductions at the gallery, though." I make my voice light like we're best friends who had a little disagreement we're ready to laugh over. "You're lucky *I* didn't throw *you* through a window."

He doesn't take the rebuke well. I went a little too far. He splutters, "Well, I wasn't–"

"Kidding." I playfully bump his shoulder again. "It's fine. I know you didn't mean it." We arrive at the side of a shiny black Mustang, the one I had picked out as his rental car. "What is the deal with the gallery, though?"

He shakes his head. "I don't think it's a good fit for you."

Asshole. I'm not surprised. I shouldn't be disappointed. I knew he would answer this way based on what just happened, yet it still hits me like an arrow to the heart. It still feels like an affront to my art. I straighten my stiff shoulders. "Right. Okay, well, I hope it works out for you."

He takes a slow survey of the parking lot, like he's getting his bearings and suddenly has no idea why he's here. His lip curls in familiar sneer. "Well. I hope this teaching thing works out for you." He infuses a world of pity and condemnation in his voice.

A few days ago that pity and condemnation might have hurt because I felt it for myself, too.

Now, though, I could not give a fuck. I've been far too wrapped up in myself and my career to see what's important. Love is what matters.

And I love Asher.

I will do anything in the world to keep him from being expelled from school and banished from the pack.

* * *

Asher

"Get in." Coach Jamison grabbed me outside and hustled me to his pickup truck.

"Coach–"

"*Get in, Asher.*" His voice is hard. Angry. But his scent has a tinge of stress in it. He's scared for me.

I climb in the cab of the pickup truck and scrub a hand over my face. "I'm done, right?"

"I don't know." He throws the car into reverse and whips out of the parking space. The entire team–Varsity and JV–stands at the gate watching us leave. He peels out when he puts it in drive. "I'm getting you off-property before anyone can make that call. I want you to get a fair trial with the council before anything's decided."

My stomach's filled with rocks. "Thanks, Coach," I mutter. "But it's all right. I was never going to make it here, anyway."

"Dammit, Asher. I would love for you to just pull your head out of your ass for three seconds and stop fighting against this pack."

I drop my head into my hands and freefall off a cliff. Because, of course, Coach is right. All this time I've been playing the part of the rebel, feeling like Lotta and the pack did my dad dirty. It defined my entire personality.

Or maybe solidified it. My dad was really the one who made me into a rebel. I rebelled against his tyranny in the ways I could growing up. But when he left, I somehow made him out to be something much better than what he was. I was missing a father figure in that crucial time of puberty and my first shift, and I'd glorified him and demo-nized the pack.

But now I know he was a louse who deserved it all. I suddenly remember and recognize what an asshole he was. How he knocked me and my mom around. Belittled us. Bullied us.

"Have you ever considered that pack members treat you

like a punk because you act like one? All you have to do is step up and be a leader. Instead of pushing against, you could be fighting *for* something. For yourself."

Coach's words are too deep for me to even process, but I close my eyes and let them wash over me. I know he cares, and it means more than I've ever let myself feel before.

In fact, I suddenly *feel everything*.

Way too much.

Shame over my behavior. Over leaving Lotta this morning. Over being such a dick to her when she was the one protecting me. Regret over not noticing that I've had an amazing father figure for the last four years–a coach who cares about me like I'm his own. Bitterness toward my dad for attacking my mate and being a shitty father and husband to my mom.

We speed up the hill toward the center of town. "You want to tell me what happened?" Coach demands.

Right.

The incident at hand. The human I just flung through a plate glass window.

"He was..." I draw a breath, trying to remember. It was all a red haze at the time. "He was touching her. She told him to stop. I–"

I have to stop and drag a deep breath in through my nostrils to quiet the red haze in front of my eyes.

"You helped him stop," Coach fills in.

I nod faintly. My focus is on the road ahead, but I'm not seeing anything.

"Okay. Call your mom. Tell her what happened, so she's not surprised by hearing it from someone else."

"Yes, Sir." My hands move mechanically, fishing my phone out and dialing my mom.

When I tell her what happened, her fear comes across the phone like a cold cocoon. "No, Asher," she whispers.

"It's okay, Mom. I'll be all right, no matter what happens."

"No... you won't. You—"

"Don't cry, Mom. It'll be okay. I love you." I'm choking up now, too, but only because I let my mom down. She doesn't deserve the shame I'm bringing on her with this. A repeat of the shame my dad brought on our family. I end the call before she can answer because there's nothing more to say.

Coach Jamison pulls in at his house and shuts off the truck. "Come on. Get inside."

I hop out of the truck. "Am I hiding?"

He blows out an exacerbated breath as he walks to the door. "Not exactly. You're in my custody. I'd rather be the guy holding you than have the sheriff get his hands on you. Or Alpha Green."

Alpha Green.

I don't expect the alpha to take mercy on me. He banished his own son for selling marijuana when he was my age. And it's not like I wasn't warned.

Coach Jamison opens the door and ushers me in. As tight as me and my friends are with Coach, he's never had us to his place. He keeps that line of respect and authority crystal clear. I look around at the small, clean house.

It's furnished simply with clean lines and modern pieces. There's a large-screen television on one wall. An apple green rug between it at the gray leather couch.

"Get cleaned up." Coach points down the hall.

"Yes, Sir."

I do as I'm told, washing the blood from my hands and

my ear. Shaking pieces of glass from my hair and clothes onto Coach's white tile floor.

When I come out, I find Coach standing in his kitchen ending a phone call.

"Well?" I ask.

"Shifter council. Tonight."

"Is it open to the rest of the pack?" I already know the answer, but I'm thinking about my mom. She would want to be there.

"No."

That means Coach Jamison can't be there either. I will have absolutely no one in my corner when I stand to speak on my own behalf. And speaking to authority has never been my gift. I am well and thoroughly fucked.

This is definitely the end of line for me in Wolf Ridge.

* * *

Lotta

"I'm sorry, Carlotta, but it's out of my hands. Alpha Green called a council meeting."

I stare at Principal Olsen, my heart beating against my ribs like a trapped bird in a cage.

I just spent two hours explaining to the principal and the sheriff exactly what happened. I worked with Zory, the janitor, to get my window outfitted with plywood. Principal Olsen made the call not to notify the school district, so he's trying to arrange for some pack members who work as builders to cover the cost of the repair.

Which doesn't help Asher's case in the slightest.

A council meeting is serious.

"That hardly seems necessary. This was a school incident, and we've taken care of the situation." I rub my nose to stop it from burning.

"I know you're sympathetic to Asher, but he has a history of unchecked volatility. While his heart was in the right place, he showed extremely poor judgment today. I hate to say it, but he's a liability to the pack. That's why I let Alpha Green know when he broke Eric Damonella's wrist, and that's why I called him again today. You know as well as I do how badly things might have gone this afternoon. If it hadn't been for your manipulation of the human, we would be looking at assault charges or a lawsuit."

"I know. But that didn't happen."

"Where is Asher now?"

I need to see my mate. Crave it with a desperation that's making me feverish. And not for sex this time. I need to know he's okay.

"Coach Jamison has him sequestered until the meeting." He looks at his watch. "But the meeting begins in ten minutes, so he'll be on his way to the pack hall."

No. I won't let Asher take the fall for this.

Especially not when all he has to do to get off is say he's my mate, and I sealed his lips on that.

I don't think he'll go against my wishes, either. He's too protective of me.

Well, dammit, I'm protective, too.

I'm going to crash that meeting.

"Will you and Coach Jamison be at the meeting?"

"No. Council only."

Fuck. "Principal Olsen?"

"Yes?"

"May I see Asher's disciplinary file?"

My employer's eyes narrow, and he considers me. I am a

teacher at the school, and Asher is my student. I believe I have a right to ask for the file, but I'm not certain.

He shrugs, though, and pulls open a drawer in the filing cabinet behind him. He hands over a folder. It's thick with handwritten and typed notes about Asher's behavior going all the way back to kindergarten. "Have at it. I can't see what good it will do you, though."

"Thank you, Sir." I take the folder and jog out to my car, leafing through the pages as I go. I have an idea. It's not fully-formed yet, but I'm hoping Asher's file will help.

* * *

Asher

The Wolf Ridge high council consists of the alpha and twelve members—six female, six male. All, including Lotta's mom, are from pack royalty—the families with the best blood lines.

Coach sits with me outside the pack hall to wait.

The door opens, and one of the pack elders nods at me to come in. There's no trace of compassion in his face.

Pack hall is designed like a courtroom with a raised dais built in a semicircle at the front of the hall. Alpha Green sits in the middle, flanked by his council members in no particular order. The room isn't opulent. Shifters aren't generally rich. It has more of an Old West feel. Like I could be strung up and hanged at dawn if they so choose.

But banishment is the worst punishment for a shifter. We're pack animals by nature. We rely on community. Once you're banished from one pack, no other will take you in. Although that's not completely true, since Garrett Green, Alpha Green's banished son, formed his own misfit pack in Tucson and is known to take in other strays.

I keep my eyes lowered as I walk in and take the single chair placed in front of the council platform.

There's a silence, no doubt intended to make me squirm.

I don't.

I'm resigned to my fate.

"Asher, you know why you're here." Alpha Green's tones hold deep disapproval." What do you have to say for yourself?"

I shake my head. "Nothing, Alpha."

"Excuse me?"

Wrong thing to say. I meant I had no excuse, but based on the thirteen frowns, they took my answer as disrespectful.

"I just mean that I did it. I deserve whatever punishment you deem fit."

Based on the sounds of disapproval, that was still the wrong answer. I guess they wanted me to grovel or something. I don't know. Diplomacy isn't an art I ever mastered.

"Well, go and wait outside while we discuss what that punishment will be," Alpha Green says.

I stand from my chair at the same time the door bursts open.

"This is a closed proceeding," Alpha Green snaps.

The scent of jasmine and honey makes me whirl to see Lotta striding into the room holding a thick manila folder. Her eyes flash with determination.

It takes everything in me not to run to her. I need to sweep her into my arms. Get everything out on the table. My apologies. My heart. What she means to me. What I'd do for her.

Kill.

Die.

Even leave, if that's what she wanted.

"I know. That's why I'm here. I have something to say related to this case."

"*Closed proceeding* means you don't get a say," her mom cries, obviously aghast at her daughter's behavior.

"No, you will hear me on this." I've never heard such strength come from Lotta. Her wolf is small. She's quiet by nature. She doesn't usually project this much power.

"*Carlotta Ann.* Get out of here right now."

"What is it?" Alpha Green asks, overriding Lotta's mom.

Lotta holds up the file in her hand triumphantly, like she's just broken Nazi codes. "I have Asher's file. A record of every disciplinary act he's been issued."

Oh, fuck. Shame burns in me. All the fights. The suspensions. The warnings. I've never been a model student.

What is she doing?

Lotta slaps the folder down on the table beside me, flashing me a quick, conspiratorial look that makes me forget my self-hatred as my heart bursts into flames.

She flips open the folder and grabs the note on top, reading from the file. "This is from third grade." She waves the piece of paper in the air, then reads from it. "Asher held John Blackmore upside down by the ankles and shook him."

My heart sinks, remembering the incident.

Lotta looks around at the council as if she's just delivered good news. "Do you want to know why?"

When no one responds, she says, "I'll tell you why! It says, *When questioned, Asher explained he was trying to shake loose the pencil John took from his friend Sebastian.*"

Clearly everyone in the room–including me–is having a *so what?* Moment.

She whips out another paper. "In fifth grade, Asher punched Nolan Sykes. Reason–Nolan pulled up the skirt of a classmate. Seventh grade–he got in a fight when someone picked on a human. Eighth grade–"

"I'm going to stop you there," Alpha Green interrupts. "What's your point?"

Lotta is undaunted by the council's disapproval.

"My point is" –she jabs a finger at the folder– "I went through that file this afternoon. There are nearly thirty incidents of violence on Asher's part and every. Single. One of them was because he was defending a weaker classmate." She points at it again. "Every one of them."

"It's not an excuse–" her mom begins, but Lotta cuts across her.

"It's *alpha wolf* behavior. It's what an alpha does. And this instinct in Asher, it should have been nurtured. It should have been encouraged and honed into leadership by this pack. By *you*." She points at Alpha Green now, and I fear he will banish the both of us.

He remains silent, though. Apparently considering her words.

She paces in front of them, like a courtroom lawyer. "Asher came from a violent household. Everyone here knows that. He wasn't safe growing up. That's the only reason I came forward and told you what his dad did to me."

"Lotta," I choke.

She meets my gaze, and I see a storm of concern and regret in those beautiful blue eyes.

"And I asked for that information to be kept secret because I wanted him to have a chance to become something different, without that hanging over his head."

I flinch.

Fuck. She was protecting me. My strong, beautiful, brave, brave mate. I hate myself for hating her.

I want to punch my own face in.

"But did anyone here step in to give him direction or help?" She scans the room with accusation.

I'm floored. Are they actually taking in her words?

"No. No, you just slapped a troublemaker label on him and assumed he'd grow up to be like his dad."

A beat of silence punctuates the scolding, then Lotta waves a hand at the folder again. "You ignored the fact that his instincts come from kindness and compassion. A sense of protecting the weaker members of his pack–the people he cares about."

I sink into my chair, not sure my legs will hold.

Lotta–my sweet mate–is defending me like no one in my life ever has.

She's reframing my reality, same as Coach did, and damn, if I don't want to live up to the potential they both see in me.

She nods. "Asher Martin is protective of me. I'm part of his pack. He defended me a few weeks ago when I was disrespected by a student, and he defended me this afternoon when I was being assaulted. He didn't know until today what his dad tried to do to me, but I know he would've tried to protect me then, too."

My nose and eyes burn, and I blink hard, looking at the floor.

"Asher is not a problem, he's a hero. And if this council would actually recognize and bring out the potential of its young pack members, instead of shaming, pigeonholing, and threatening to throw them out, then more of us young people might be willing to stick around." She sets her jaw and meets her mother's gaze, and I want to clap my hands and cheer.

There is no slow-clap though. Alpha Green takes back his council meeting. "Thank you. We've heard enough," he says to Lotta. "Wait outside." He looks at me.

"Yes, Alpha." I stand.

"I know you'll do the right thing," Lotta says loudly as she walks out ahead of me.

The moment I close the door behind us, I pull Lotta into my arms in a silent embrace. My nose burns, and my throat constricts. "Lotta," I whisper-choke against her hair.

"I love you, Asher," she whispers back.

I release her enough to cradle her face, tracing the curve of her cheeks with my thumbs. "I love you so much. I always have."

Her eyes swim. "You know what?" Tears choke her voice. "Fuck it. Let me make this absolutely clear."

She shoves the door to the council back open and grabs my hand, tugging me back in with her.

"I said wait outside," the alpha booms.

Lotta is undaunted. "Just one more thing–Asher is my mate." She holds up our joined hands. "So if he goes, I go. Just wanted to make that clear."

* * *

Lotta

I fall back against the door laughing. Asher tugs me into his arms, kissing all over my face. He palms my ass, lifting me so my legs wrap around his waist as he deepens the kiss. We're making out against the door to the council meeting that will determine our fate.

Both of our fates.

Because they are now forever intertwined.

"I want you to mark me," I pant, rocking against the bulge in his jeans.

"Oh, I'm going to, sweetheart." His tongue plunges into my mouth. He drags his open mouth across my jaw. "I'm going to mark the ever-living-fuck out of you."

I laugh.

"I'm going to mark you with my teeth"–he bites my neck–"and my scent"–he slides one hand under my shirt to cup my breast–"and my cum." His straining cock presses in the notch between my legs. "I'm going to mark you with my fingers." Said fingers slide over my panties over the crack of my ass.

"Lotta." He slows his movements and holds my gaze. "Baby, I'm so sorry about this morning. I'm really ashamed that I wolfed out and ran."

I hold his face between my two hands. "No. Of course you did. You were shocked and upset."

"Baby, *no*." He leans his forehead against mine. We're connected in so many places–hips, heads, hands, but most importantly–hearts. "You're the one who has a reason and a right to be upset. I should've been there for you. I should've...held you." He swallows. I sense the tension in his body. "I should've apologized."

I get the feeling apologies don't come easy for Asher.

"I already know you're sorry," I tell him. "I feel your suffering. I feel it like my own." I slide my fingers through his golden waves. It feels so incredible to be aligned with Asher after all our messy prior attempts. We needed this crisis to bring us together. Make us realize what's important and what isn't.

"All this time, I thought my dilemma was between my wolf side and my artist side. I thought I had to stay away from Wolf Ridge, or it would stop my career. But now that all feels irrelevant. My wolf wanted me back here to find you. My artist side did, too. You're my destiny, Asher. My tomorrow. My forever."

"You're my everything." He kisses me, lips slanting across mine, tongue sliding between my lips.

A throat clears on the other side of the door, and we pull apart, both gasping.

I let out a breathy laugh as Asher pulls me away from the door and drops me to my feet.

When he opens the door, we find my mom standing there. "Come back in. Both of you." There's high color in her cheeks, but I can't read her agitation.

Asher squeezes my hand as we enter the council room.

Alpha Green beckons us forward. "We've reached a decision." He does the power move of letting silence descend for a moment before he delivers his sentence.

"Carlotta, I found your defense of Asher thought-provoking, and I do take your criticism of my leadership to heart. I've made mistakes as an alpha. And you're right, perhaps if I had done things differently, population wouldn't be declining in Wolf Ridge."

I suspect he's referring to his banishment of his own son from the pack when he was just eighteen.

"Asher, your instincts do seem to be good, as Carlotta pointed out. But you need to learn restraint. You endanger this pack every time you act impulsively."

"Yes, Alpha." Asher takes the rebuke like a man.

"We believe your fated mate will help with the temperance. While we understand the impropriety of your relationship given that Carlotta is a teacher at Wolf Ridge High this semester, we're ordering you to claim her immediately.

It's too volatile for an alpha wolf to hold off on marking his mate."

Asher shoots me a concerned look.

I squeeze his hand. If I lose this job, I lose it. My future is Asher.

"The two of you will keep the relationship secret from all humans until Asher has graduated."

"So...I can remain in the art teacher position?"

"Yes. Wolf Ridge High needs your talent," Alpha Green says. If my mom had said it, I wouldn't believe her. I would assume she was just saying that to keep me here. But considering I just threw down over them not recognizing our talents, I'm willing to receive his words as genuine appreciation. Or an attempt at genuine appreciation, anyway.

"That's all. You're both dismissed."

I look up at Asher and find he's grinning down at me, dimples at full setting, looking transformed. I laugh when he scoops me up into his arms and carries me out on exuberant steps. When we bust out of the pack hall, he spins me in circles, lowering and lifting me like I'm on an amusement park ride. I shriek with laughter, my arms tight around his neck, my joy exploding from my chest.

"Let's go, sweetheart. You heard the alpha. I've been ordered to claim you. And it's gonna be good."

Chapter Twenty-Two

sher

Carlotta lit candles again. I picked up take-out containers from the deli for later. Right now I'm taking my time with her. I tied her spread eagle to the bed, and I'm kissing every inch of her pale skin.

She trembles beneath me, tugging at the bonds, shivering in response.

"You want my tongue here?" I nip her inner thigh, close to her sex.

"Yes." She arches, sending her pebbled nipples toward the ceiling. I fondle one, brushing the pad of my finger over the tip as I flick my tongue closer to where she needs me. "Please," she warbles.

"You'll get your pleasure when I decide, sweetheart." I remind her who's in charge. Not because I still need to be but because she deserves to let go. To not have to worry about anything. To lie back and receive.

I'll never forget what she did for me tonight. No one has ever stood up for me like that before and damn if I don't want to be the male she thinks I am—a leader. Her protector. The alpha to a pack.

"This little body belongs to me now." I brush my thumb over the seam of her pussy with a feather touch.

She bucks for more.

"I'm the guy who gets to give you pleasure. No one else." I suddenly remember the events of this afternoon, which feel like a lifetime ago. "Who the fuck was that guy today, anyway?" I can't help the growl of jealousy from lacing my voice.

"He was one of my roommates in Chicago. I used him for sex sometimes because I needed it, and it was convenient, but we were never even friends. He's an asshole."

"He came here for sex?" I try to keep my roar of anger out of my voice.

"You protected me," Lotta soothes.

It works. My wolf settles, and logic returns to my brain. "You could've protected yourself, of course. I'm sorry I lost control like that."

"No, it wasn't your fault. The alpha is right. It was because you haven't marked me. And because of what you learned this morning."

Right. That. "I don't want that to interfere with our night. But tomorrow, You'll tell me what happened. Everything."

"Okay. Of course, yes."

I lift my head to meet her gaze. "Are you really mine? You want me to mark you?"

"Yes, Asher. When I thought you were going to be banished, I realized that I couldn't stand that. I can't be apart from you. You're all that matters."

I shake my head. "Not true. Your hopes and dreams

matter, too. Your art. You wanted to leave Wolf Ridge. We can. I'll go with you. Anywhere."

Her lips part, but no words come out.

"Coach said I might have a shot at UCLA. Would Los Angeles have a better art scene?"

Her eyes shine. "Yes. Yes–that would be amazing."

"Then we'll make it happen." I slide my hands under her ass and lift her core to my mouth. I lick into her, parting her sweet flesh, tracing the insides of her lips. I get my lips over her tiny clit and suck.

She comes immediately, tugging at the ropes I used to tie her. "Inside. Please. I need you inside me."

I tsk. "I didn't say you could come, beautiful. I think a little punishment is in order."

"Oh, fate," she moans. "Please, Asher. I need you so badly."

I chuckle, her words making my entire being pulse with warmth and pleasure. "Not yet, beautiful. You're going to take my dick in your gorgeous ass, my fingers in your sweet pussy, and my teeth in that delectable shoulder."

She bucks some more, another little orgasm running through her.

"This body was made for me, wasn't it?" I work on untying her wrists. "Hm?"

"You're mine, too, Asher," Lotta murmurs. There's a sense of wonder on her face, like she just realized it.

"I am," I agree as I untie her ankles. "I am your warrior. I will wage war on your behalf. I will level anyone who stands in your way."

Lotta laughs. "I know you would. Even when you hated me, I knew you'd do anything for me."

The smile falls away from my face, remembering all that

hate I directed her way. I work to swallow. "I'm so sorry about that."

"No, no. I realized this morning that we needed things to go the way they did. You needed to believe I'd wronged you because it made you tough and strong. It made you into the warrior you are. And I needed to run away from who I was and suppress my wolf, so she would come out through my paintings and show me my future. With you." Hands now free, Lotta reaches for my face and holds it between her two hands. "You are my future, Asher. Don't you see? There were no mistakes. Everything led us to now. To this moment. To whom we've become apart and together. Both of us needed to go into the crucible, so we'd arrive here."

I smash my mouth over Lotta's in a rough, passionate kiss. And now I've forgotten the nuanced sex I planned for us.

The need to claim her, to consummate us and this moment is too strong.

Before I know what I'm doing, I've pushed her onto her back on the bed, my hand cradled behind her head, my tongue exploring her mouth.

I knock her knees wide and find home, piercing her with a brutal thrust.

"Oh, fate, yes." She throws her head back, rocking up to take me even deeper.

I don't break the kiss. It's like I'm trying to express the depth of my passion for her with every twist of my lips. Every thrust of my tongue. I want her more than I've ever wanted anything in my life. I need to consume her. To marry her. To mark and mate her.

The bed slams against the wall with the force of my thrusts. The mattress bows and springs.

I grip the headboard with one hand and drive into her like our lives depend on it.

"Yes, yes!" Lotta cries.

"Yes." I don't recognize my own voice, it's so deep and guttural.

There's a moment when we transcend. I swear we dip into a space of no time and place. Of infinity. Of experiencing the fractals of every lifetime and dimension we've been mates.

There's a roaring in my ears. Like rushing water or wind. I shout, but I can't hear my voice over the noise.

All I know is I'm coming.

Lotta's already there.

The moment expands and widens. It crystallizes.

Serum coats my teeth before they sink into her shoulder, forever embedding my scent in her skin.

We both orgasm again.

When I finally withdraw my teeth from her shoulder and lick the wounds closed, I murmur, "I love you, Lotta James."

"I love you, Asher Martin. Forever and always."

* * *

Lotta

"What happened here?" I ask in the shower the next morning, my fingertips tracing the jagged marks of a recent trauma.

I woke in Asher's arms again–pure heaven, if shifters believed in heaven. We made love in the warm sheets, and I told him the story of what happened with his dad. It killed him, but he stayed present. Held me. Listened. Cried.

I promised I wasn't traumatized. That my only trauma had ever been over hurting him.

Then he carried me here, to the shower, where we made love again. If this is my life now, I love it.

"What?" Asher looks down at his torso and swipes a hand over the healing wounds.

How did I not notice them last night? I was too swept away to even realize my mate was hurt.

"Oh. I got hit by a car yesterday."

"Asher!"

"No, it was a good thing. I was out of my mind, running up through bear country. Getting hit on the highway knocked the sense back into me. That's what made me realize I'd screwed up leaving you."

The part of me that believed I had to muscle through life and do everything on my own relaxes even more. I'm still getting used to the idea that I'll never be alone again. That someone will always have my back.

"I love you." I can't say the words enough. Every time I say them or hear them, a new wick is lit inside me. The flames grow stronger. Brighter.

Asher flashes me that dimpled smile that makes my knees weak as he loops an arm behind my back and pulls me up against him. "Say it again."

"I love you."

"One more time."

"I love you."

His kiss is soft and giving. "I want to turn the world inside out for you."

The wings around my heart beat faster.

He turns off the water and pulls open the shower curtain. "And that starts with getting you to your job on time." He grabs a towel from the rack and wraps me in it.

"And while I will hate pretending at school, I can't fucking wait for every shifter in Wolf Ridge to know you belong to me."

I laugh. "You're crazy."

"Yep. Crazy for you."

* * *

Asher

There's a fuck-ton of whispering about me when I walk into the school. Which makes sense because I'm sure the entire town heard by now that I threw a guy out of the art studio window.

I had to do the same sneak-of-shame out of Carlotta's place and drive separately on my motorcycle, which I hated, but that doesn't dampen my pride. I marked my mate. Lotta belongs to me in the eyes of the pack. Every shifter will know she's been claimed.

Of course, no one can tell by my scent anything has changed.

Maybe they will by my swagger. By my smile. By the lift of my sternum and the openness of my chest.

My inner pack–Abe, J. J., Markley and Seb–is all over me, crowding around my locker.

"What the fuck, bro?" Abe gives me a friendly shove. "I literally lit up your phone last night. You couldn't just text me back to let me know you're still in the fucking pack?"

"Yeah, dude," Seb says. "Asshole. We even went over to see your mom last night, and she didn't know anything."

Right. My poor mom. I did call her after the council meeting to give her the news, so she didn't suffer all night like my friends.

"You no-showed to school and practice then drove up

and threw a guy through a window yesterday. What is going on with you?" J. J. demands.

I grin. "Yeah, sorry. I was, uh, kinda busy."

"Busy doing what?" Abe demands.

"Marking my mate."

A slow smile spreads across Abe's face. "No shit."

"*What mate?*" J. J. demands. Abe obviously kept my secret, even after what happened yesterday.

"Carlotta James," Abe can't help himself now. He offers me a fist to bump.

"Hottie Lottie," Markley says.

"Call her that again, and I'll rip your tongue out," I say, but I'm too happy to sound like I mean it.

The insane jealousy and possessiveness has been soothed by the knowledge that she's mine now.

"What, it's true. You're lucky, bruh. So lucky. You found your fated mate. Both of you did. While still in high school. What are the fucking chances?" Markley says.

"One in a million." Abe catches sight of his gorgeous mate walking down the hall, and his grin gets as cocky as mine. He fist-bumps me again. "Gotta go. Congratulations."

"So you're not banished or suspended?" J. J. asks when Abe leaves.

"Nope. Just ordered to mark her and keep it a secret from humans."

"Lucky bastard."

"Seriously. Lucky as fuck." Markley sounds jealous. Finding your one true fated mate is something most of us are programmed to believe won't happen for us. But maybe that's just council propaganda to make us stay in Wolf Ridge and not go out searching.

Eric Damonella walks by, still wearing the useless cast I subjected him to. He casts me a quick, nervous glance.

"Hey, man," I say, willing to be benevolent now that Lotta's mine.

He stops, relief obvious in his shoulders. "Hey."

"I'm not gonna apologize because I'm not sorry, but we're cool. So long as you never look at or speak about my mate again."

His eyes bulge. "Your mate?"

I nod, satisfaction ricocheting through my chest. "You heard me. Make sure everyone knows it. Anyone disrespects her, they die."

He falls backward a step. "You got it, Asher. No problem."

I grab my books for first period, and then the world goes slow-mo. A chica-bow-wow song plays in my head, and I stop to drink in the sight of my gorgeous mate walking down the hall, tossing her raven black hair over her shoulder and giving me a secret look.

Fuck. Me.

My life could not get any better.

Chapter Twenty-Three

Lotta

Asher smirks at me from his customary seat in the back row.

My heart pounds with excitement every time he enters. I can feel the blast of love from him. His attention remains riveted to my face or body the entire lesson, even when he should be working. He listens now when I lecture–to every word. He won't let anyone speak over me or talk back to me.

I made Asher glue the necklace back on his self-portrait, and I keep it propped in the window beside my desk, so I can look at it all day long.

We make a game out of sneaking around at school. Asher's put me on my hands and knees on this desk. He's claimed me in the supply closet. We've returned to the staff bathroom a few times. Right now he's giving me a tiny smile. One that implies all the dirty things he's going to do to me later.

Tonight, I'm going to show him how much he means not just to me, but to everyone in this pack.

I finish up my lecture and give them the assignment for

the next project. "Any questions? No? All right. Have a good weekend. I will see you Monday."

The bell rings and students file out. Asher hangs back.

"Did you have a question, Asher?" I use my prim teacher voice.

It gets Asher hard. He adjusts himself as he stands and saunters up to me. "I have something to show you, Ms. James." He pulls an envelope from his book and drops it on my desk. It's addressed to me but with his home address.

The return address is Swan Hotel Corporation.

"What is this?" I flip it over and open the flap. Inside I find a letter.

Dear Ms. James,

Congratulations! We have selected you as the recipient of our prestigious Swan Art Award and artist-in-residence program. As you know, during the six-month residency, the ten pieces of artwork you submitted will hang in the lobby of our Los Angeles headquarters. In exchange, you will receive a stipend of twenty-five thousand dollars, and a fully furnished apartment and studio to continue creating work.

Enclosed are the details. To accept our award, please fill out the paperwork and return to us no later than November 15th.

We look forward to making arrangements to install you and your art next fall.

Best Regards,
    Bea Daily
    Director, Swan Art Award Program

. . .

My hand trembles. "What is this?" I repeat, dazed.

"I've been entering your artwork to contests. Lauren Sterling connected me with an art gallery owner who said the way to gain recognition was to submit to these kinds of things. She gave me a list, and I've been sending photos and descriptions of your work everywhere."

My eyes fill with tears. "What? Since when?"

"Since the meadow. When we realized your art was prophetic. I knew it was important to try to support you in this, especially since your family hasn't."

"Asher." I throw my arms around him and squeeze him tight. "This is incredible. I can't believe it."

He grins. "You're happy."

"Is there any doubt?"

"I called the coach at UCLA and said they were my top choice. I just figured it doesn't hurt to let them know I'm interested. Some ballers are playing hard ball with them to get more. I just want a spot." He shrugs. "I'm pretty sure they'll find me money and a spot."

"Incredible!"

"Yep. Our future–away from here–is right around the corner."

I shake my head. "I don't even care about moving anymore. But yes. And Wolf Ridge will be here if we want to come back."

"Yeah. Good. My mom is gonna want to hold our pups."

I laugh. I notice my instinct to shut him down on pups, since I've been doing it forever with my mom, but then it morphs into something different.

Oh.

I definitely do want pups. I want to see Asher as a dad. I

want to create a family with him. And yes, I might want to move back here. But after we've gone out to conquer the world.

Together.

Always together.

With Asher by my side, I believe we can do anything we set our minds to.

Epilogue

Asher

  I pump the keg and dispense another two beers for myself and Lotta. There's a party up on the mesa to celebrate our send-off. Our age difference makes for an interesting mix of people at the party. It's mostly my friends–other graduates–but also some of Lotta's friends, like Olive and Brianna.

Lotta and I leave tomorrow for Los Angeles for her artist in residency.

Last weekend was graduation.

I'm not the kind of guy who ever pictured walking on graduation day with the cap and gown and all that shit.

It's not something I was working toward. I guess because I wasn't focused on what came after.

Now that I have an after–an *ever after*–with Lotta, it feels important.

Lotta was up on the stage today when I picked up my diploma and shook Principal Olsen and Coach Jamison's hand. My mom and Mrs. Angelson were in the stands crying.

Lotta's parents were there, too.

It took a little while, but they warmed up to me. And once they did, they were all in. My mom and I were invited to dinner every other week. I think Lotta's mom was hoping to persuade us to stay in Wolf Ridge. She wants grandpups.

We had it out a couple of weeks ago when it felt like she kept shitting all over Lotta's artist-in-residency. I told her that her lack of support for Lotta's art career was disappointing to me, and I hoped she would do better for her grandpups when they came around.

That got her. She burst into tears and apologized to my mate. It was pretty beautiful, actually.

I'm shooting the shit with Seb over the keg when I hear a huge chorus of "Coach!" and I turn in surprise.

Coach never parties with us. He's very good about keeping the lines clear. He's not our friend or buddy. He's an elder who deserves our unwavering respect. So for him to show up to the party is a shock.

Of course, my first assumption is that I'm in trouble.

Lifelong habit, I guess.

"Coach." I stride forward and shake his hand, then offer him a beer.

To my shock, he takes it.

"No offense, Coach, but what are you doing here?"

Coach tips his head toward Lotta. "Your mate asked me to come and say a few words."

I stare at Lotta blankly. "She did?"

Lotta slides up behind me, wrapping her slender arms around my waist. "C'mere, beautiful." I tug her around to my side, so I can loop an arm around her. "What is this about?"

"I asked Coach Jamison here tonight because I know

how much his mentorship has meant to you. And we're going to do something."

"Do something?" I ask blankly.

"Yep." I see a happy secret in Lotta's expression, and it feels like I'm being lifted by a thousand helium balloons, my weight growing lighter and lighter until I'm surprised my feet still touch the earth.

It's everything to see her so easy. So happy. That tortured artist look has been replaced by free-spiritedness.

"Coach Jamison, will you get everyone's attention?"

Coach lifts his thumb and middle finger to his mouth and whistles loud enough to make everyone stop talking.

Lotta waves a hand in the air. "Hey everyone," she calls out.

I lift her up by the waist and carry her to stand on a boulder to give her the height she lacks. "Thank you all for coming out to see us off tonight. I wanted to say a few words before we go."

Our friends smile and raise their cups.

"Leaving Wolf Ridge can be hard. We're pack animals. Our survival is baked around community. You probably know that less than twenty percent of Wolf Ridge grads leave and probably half of those are human. Leaving my pack and my kind was hard for me. My parents didn't want me to go. They tried to block me from leaving by withdrawing all financial support, so when I left, it felt more like a jailbreak than a graduation."

Our friends laugh.

"I didn't want that for Asher. I don't expect it will be, though. In a way, he's been without pack, or on the wrong side of the pack, since his father's banishment."

I wince hearing it spoken out loud, so publicly. But there's something freeing about it, too. The shame I carried all those years is being aired out under the pine trees. My close friends–Abe, Markley, J.J. and Seb, will still be my friends. They always have been. And I don't care about the rest of them.

"That's why I invited you all to contribute to his send-off. So he'd be leaving on the wings of the pack, not fleeing in the night, like I did."

I look around, still not getting it. But that's when I see J.J. walking around with a shoebox, holding it out for people to throw envelopes in.

"Oh no," I say, fearing it's some kind of fundraiser. My pride kicks in. "What is this?"

"They're letters." Coach Jamison produces a stack of letters from his back pocket and starts leafing through them. "I have one here from the alpha, from your mom, the mailman, your next door neighbor, some of your teachers."

"Letters."

"There's one from me, too. You can save it for when you need a pep talk/kick in the ass from your old coach, though."

J.J. passes in front of Coach, and he drops his stack of letters into the cardboard box.

My eyes start to burn. I recapture Lotta from the rock because I need to hold her in my arms to keep me steady. She straddles my waist, arms looped around my neck.

"Your mate is making sure you know you're important here. You matter. The pack should've done better by you, and Lotta gave them a chance to rectify that situation. You have an entire box full of letters from people who care about you–old and young."

"Fuck," I mutter, stumbling back.

"Indeed," Coach says, for once not calling me on the bad language. He takes the box from J. J. and hands it to me with a clap on the back. "Next time you start feeling like the world's against you, pull out a letter and read it. This pack belongs to you, and you belong to it. Even when you're gone."

Lotta squeezes me tight, and I realize she's crying.

I lower her to her feet and cradle her beautiful face. "You okay?"

"Yeah," she lets out a watery laugh. "That just hit hard, you know? Because that's what I didn't know when I was gone the first time. I didn't realize I still belonged somewhere, and I still had support, even if it didn't come from my parents, who had their heads stuck up their asses."

I blink rapidly against the moisture in my eyes. "Yeah, I can see that."

I thumb away her tears, then slant my lips over hers to kiss her softly. "Thank you, angel. What you did was incredible. A gift I'll have for the rest of my life."

"You're welcome."

"But the best gift of all is always gonna be you."

Lotta blinks her own tears back. "No, you," she says impishly.

"You."

She squirms out of my arms and takes off running. "You!" she calls over her shoulder.

Every pack member knows exactly what she's inciting. Clothing flies in every direction. There are flashes of fur–black, tan, white, grey, and every mix possible of the colors as we all transform into wolves, boys chasing girls. Girls chasing boys.

The full moon claiming all of us in a silvery baptism of light.

I stay on Lotta's heels, following, but not overpowering. Not yet.

Not until I find the perfect place to throw her down and fuck her hard.

And then to cradle her close and keep her.

Forever, mine.

* * *

Thank you for reading Alpha Varsity. If you enjoyed it, **I would so appreciate your review**. They make a huge difference for indie authors like me.

If you're not already a member, I'd love to see you in **my Facebook Group, Renee's Romper Room.**

Here's the playlist to go along with Alpha Varsity! <3

https://open.spotify.com/playlist/771hEIk5zlII7dl l22obJQ?si=90de8a05c2c94I5a

Want FREE books?

Go to http://subscribepage.com/alphastemp to sign up for Renee Rose's newsletter and receive a free books. In addition to the free stories, you will also get special pricing, exclusive previews and news of new releases.

Other Titles by Renee Rose

Alpha's Vow

Alpha's Revenge

Alpha's Fire

Alpha's Rescue

Alpha's Command

Werewolves of Wall Street

Big Bad Boss: Midnight

Big Bad Boss: Moon Mad

Big Bad Boss: Marked

Big Bad Boss: Mated

Alpha Doms Series

The Alpha's Hunger

The Alpha's Promise

The Alpha's Punishment

The Alpha's Protection (Dirty Daddies)

Two Marks Series

Untamed

Tempted

Desired

Enticed

Wolf Ranch Series

Rough

Wild

Feral

Savage

Warrior

Vegas Underground Mafia Romance

King of Diamonds

Mafia Daddy

Jack of Spades

Ace of Hearts

Joker's Wild

His Queen of Clubs

Dead Man's Hand

Wild Card

Daddy Rules Series

Fire Daddy

Hollywood Daddy

Stepbrother Daddy

Master Me Series

Her Royal Master

Her Russian Master

Her Marine Master

Yes, Doctor

Double Doms Series

Theirs to Punish

Theirs to Protect

Holiday Feel-Good

Scoring with Santa

Saved

Other Contemporary

Black Light: Valentine Roulette

Black Light: Roulette Redux

Black Light: Celebrity Roulette

Black Light: Roulette War

Black Light: Roulette Rematch

Punishing Portia (written as Darling Adams)

The Professor's Girl

Safe in his Arms

Sci-Fi
Zandian Masters Series

His Human Slave

His Human Prisoner

Training His Human

His Human Rebel

His Human Vessel

His Mate and Master

Zandian Pet

Their Zandian Mate

His Human Possession

Zandian Brides

Night of the Zandians

Bought by the Zandians

Mastered by the Zandians

About Renee Rose

USA TODAY BESTSELLING AUTHOR RENEE ROSE loves a dominant, dirty-talking alpha hero! She's sold over two million copies of steamy romance with varying levels of kink. Her books have been featured in USA Today's *Happily Ever After* and *Popsugar*. Named Eroticon USA's Next Top Erotic Author in 2013, she has also won *Spunky and Sassy's* Favorite Sci-Fi and Anthology author, *The Romance Reviews* Best Historical Romance, and has hit the *USA Today* list fifteen times with her Bad Boy Alphas, Chicago Bratva, and Wolf Ranch series.

Renee loves to connect with readers!
www.reneeroseromance.com
reneeroseauthor@gmail.com

 facebook.com/reneeroseromance

instagram.com/reneeroseromance

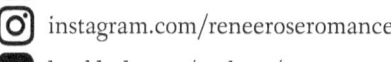 bookbub.com/authors/renee-rose